THE OPTICIAN OF LAMPEDUSA

THE OPTICIAN OF LAMPEDUSA

BASED ON A TRUE STORY

EMMA JANE KIRBY

OR Books

New York · London

© 2017 Emma Jane Kirby

Published for the book trade by OR Books in partnership with Counterpoint Press, by arrangement with Éditions des Equateurs.
Distributed to the trade by Publishers Group West

Visit our website at www.orbooks.com

North American rights information: rights@orbooks.com

First US trade printing 2017.

Cataloging-in-Publication data is available from the Library of Congress.

ISBN 978-1-94486-915-1

Text design by Under|Over. Typeset by AarkMany Media, Chennai, India.

10 9 8 7 6 5 4 3 2 1

FOREWORD

I first met the Optician of Lampedusa when I was making a series of radio programs for the BBC on how ordinary Italians had been affected by the migration crisis. We were aware that our listeners were feeling saturated with the migration story and had begun to switch off from it, so we were keen to find a way to recall their attention to the enormity of this news story. We interviewed four Italians who were all actively involved with the migrants' plight: a hospital director, a gravedigger, a house-wife turned soup kitchen chef, and a carpenter who carved wooden crosses from the wrecks of the migrants' boats, offering them to survivors as a symbol of hope and new life. Our last interviewee, the Optician, was not a volunteer. He saw the migrants every day and felt pity for them but, like most of us, he figured they were not his problem.

On October 3, 2013, the Optician of Lampedusa, who was taking a boating holiday with his wife and friends, found himself in the middle of the biggest shipwreck that the little Italian island had ever seen. Hundreds of drowning people were in the water screaming for help with their last breath. And it was at that moment that the Optician understood that it was no longer an option to stay a spectator on the sidelines. He realized the migration crisis was just as much his problem as anyone else's.

"It was me on the boat that day," he told me. "But tomorrow?"

Shortly after writing this book, I was invited to report from the Labanof Pathology Laboratory in Milan, where a forensic team was trying to identify the 368 victims of the tragedy. I was shown a photograph album, containing close-up images of the drowned. I will never forget those swollen, bruised faces. Their ship went down just eight hundred meters from shore; survivors said they could see car taillights on the mainland. Many excited asylum seekers had gone below deck to change clothes to be smart for their arrival in the Promised Land of Europe. It was then that a man lit a towel to attract attention to their drifting boat. The fire took hold across one side of the deck and the migrants ran to the other side. The boat lolled under their weight and tipped over.

"There were just too many people in the water," the Optician remembered. "My first thought was, how do I save them all?" The Optician of Lampedusa rarely gives interviews. He is haunted by the tragedy. I asked him how that day on the sea changed him and he looked me straight in the eye.

"Whenever I have a bad day," he said, "I remember that I have a little house, a little family, that I have my little business. And I say to myself: you are not in the water."

This book is based on the true story of Carmine Menna, the Optician of Lampedusa.

—Emma Jane Kirby
London, June 2016

PROLOGUE

I could hardly begin to describe to you what I saw as our boat approached the source of that terrible noise. I hardly want to. You wouldn't understand because you weren't there. You couldn't understand. You see, I thought I'd heard seagulls screeching. Seagulls fighting over a lucky catch. Birds. Just birds.

We were in the open sea after all. It couldn't have been anything else.

I had never seen so many people in the water. Their limbs were thrashing, hands grasping, fists punching, black faces flashing over them under the waves. Gasping, yelling, choking, screaming. Oh God, the screaming! The pitch of it! The sea boiling and writhing around them as they kicked and lashed out, clinging to each other, grabbing at pieces of driftwood, snatching handfuls of water as they tried to clutch the tops of the breakers. They were in a frenzy of desperation, shrieking at us, trying to attract our attention on the little boat. And they were scattered everywhere—in every direction I turned there was another of them, hundreds of them, plunging, spluttering, an outstretched arm, beating the water, pleading. And my wife, sobbing my name, sobbing my name as the propeller of the motor cut a jagged, clumsy path through the bodies.

They were all drowning. I thought: how do I save them all?

I can still feel the fingers of that first hand I seized. How they cemented into mine, bone grinding against bone, how they clamped down with such a grip that I saw the sinuous veins of the wrist pounding. The force of the hold! My hand in a stranger's hand, in a bond stronger and more intimate than an umbilical cord. And my whole body shook with the force of that hold as I pulled upward and dragged the naked torso from the waves.

There were too many of them. Too many of them and I didn't know what to do. I'm an Optician; I'm not a lifesaver. I'm an Optician and I was on vacation and I didn't know what to do.

I threw the rubber ring but there were people strewn like wreckage over a five-hundred-meter radius and they were all crying out for us. I reached over the stern step again and again but there were so many hands shooting out from beneath the waves, so many hands snatching at the air. My fingers locked on to fingers and I pulled.

Were we sinking? The boat was so low in the water. Someone shouted at me but I couldn't stop to listen. There were too many hands. The deck was crammed with black bodies vomiting and defecating all over each other. I could feel the boat protesting under the weight, rolling, ready to flip over. I knew the boat was out of control.

Over there! Another hand!

I never wanted to tell you this story. I promised myself I would never tell this story again because it's not a fairy tale. There were just too many of them. I wanted to go back for them. I wanted to go back.

Do you understand what I'm trying to say to you? Maybe it's not possible for you to understand because you weren't in that boat. But I was there and I saw them. I still see them. Because it's still happening.

CHAPTER 1

The Optician of Lampedusa was running. With each footfall, small puffs of dust rose up from the cracked road and the tiny particles swirled in a fine, rust-colored haze around his knees. There was little wind today, even on the coastal road; it wheezed across the Optician's face in dry, irregular gasps and he could smell the tang of the sea on its briny breath. It was almost too hot to be running under this glaring autumn sun but he kept pushing forward, the dirt clotting in patches on his legs as it mingled with his sweat. Somewhere, perhaps from the port at the mouth of the town, he could hear a dog howling. Whatever time of day or night on this island, he thought, there's always a stray dog barking somewhere.

It was more Africa here than Italy, really. Running here, away from the gelato and cappuccino bars and the souvenir shops of the little town, you could imagine you were in Africa, especially when you passed a little stone-walled *dammuso* with its whitewashed roof. He screwed up his eyes. You could almost see the African coast from here. Tunisia, Lampedusa's nearest neighbor, was twice as close as Sicily.

For twenty-five years now he has lived in this dry, arid landscape. For twenty-five years he has been running through this craggy, barren scrubland, getting scratched by its thorn bushes and caked with its grime. This calm was so different from the agitated chaos of his native Naples but the Optician had never regretted exchanging his sprawling city for the solitude of this little island. It may have been only ten square kilometers long, perhaps half the size of Naples, but with Lampedusa, he had sea on all sides. The Optician needed the sea.

He looked at the water as he jogged along the tracks of the island's south coast. Splintered cobalt and turquoise as bright and smooth as cheap jewelry and he knew that if he were to dive into it now, even though today was the first day of October, it would still be warm and welcoming. Out on the boat with his wife, Teresa, he watched dolphins and sometimes sperm whales swimming in the tranquil waters. He and Teresa often swam at the paradisiacal Rabbit Beach, where the bleached sands radiated heat and where occasional shoals of parrot fish splashed color across the white canvas as they flitted and darted across the bay in the fractured light. In the summer, the rare loggerhead turtles chose these beaches to lay their eggs. His wife said it was because Nature recognized that Lampedusa would always be gentle with whatever washed up here.

The Optician's feet pounded on. The heat caused a knotted vein just above his right ear to pulse and he could trace it throbbing across his bald head and up into his skull. He liked to push himself, to feel his body working. He had always been slim and fit. Years ago, he had enjoyed the physical discipline of his military service and although he might have been in his late fifties now, he wouldn't let anything slip.

A teenager roared past him on an old scooter, the rowdy engine shattering the silence of his run. He watched the boy weaving pointless tire trails in and out of the dust, wheeling and revving the bike. There wasn't much for youth to do here in the evenings—a handful of bars and cafes, a small club with a karaoke machine. His own parents hadn't wanted him hanging around Naples when he'd left school, didn't want him getting bored and into trouble. They'd sent him to a tailoring college where he'd learned how to cut made-to-measure suits. He'd become famous for his exactness and precision. He smiled to himself. He'd known it was never really going to satisfy him in the long term though, not when he was nurturing a secret ambition to become an Optician. A strange passion for a young man, you might think; but he had always been fascinated by sight, by how and what people saw. So alongside his tailoring, he had studied optics.

A small group of African men shuffled toward him down the road into town. He lifted a hand to them as he passed them and they muttered a shy greeting in return. He wondered if they had arrived on the island this morning—almost every day now he saw the buses leaving the port packed with newly arrived migrants. They hung out by the supermarket opposite his shop and he saw crowds of them clustered around the church. Maybe they were very Christian in whatever part of Africa they came from? His neighbors collected food and stuff for them; there was always someone rattling a tin. A woman, presumably from the parish, had called round that morning asking if he had any old clothes or shoes to donate but he'd been drowning in paper-work and hadn't had time to stop. Apparently the migrant center was full to bursting again; maybe that's why they preferred to wander the island like this.

Crazy, he thought, that they all turned up here when this country had precious little to offer them. There was many a moment over the last few years when he thought his own business was going under; how many sleepless nights did he and Teresa have over that? He exhaled noisily. Everything he had worked so damn hard for was threatened! He felt his heart rate increase to keep pace with his rising temper. The town hall here was constantly yanking up the business rates until he was half-strangled by taxes and fees and duties and God knows what else. It felt as if he was always being hounded and tapped for money by some official or other.

He faced the low sun. He saw little colored sparks of red and gold and green when he blinked and he put a hand up to shield himself from the glare. He should have worn sunglasses. The lights flashed and fizzed around his eyes.

He worried for his two sons mostly, of course. He needed to make sure they were provided for, because frankly how on earth they would find long-term jobs in this shrinking economy he did not know. They were bright lads, both of them, and hard workers, too. The eldest wanted to set up his own business; he had a real entrepreneurial spirit, that one. But it was a risk, of course. Being self-employed was always a risk, as he knew all too well.

But he could not imagine working for anyone else now; it would be unthinkable. His gaze swept from left to right. Being master of himself, master of his own time, managing his own little world—that's what he liked. And no one could say he didn't put the hours in: he worked hard during the week keeping his little business thriving for his family. Then his reward—he looked back over his shoulder toward the sea again—his reward was having all this wonderful nature as his own playground.

The seagulls began mewing excitedly and the Optician looked upward to watch them flock and circle over the coast. He knew they were waiting for the last of the fishing trawlers to head back to port, hoping to pick up scraps. If he could time his run right, he would be back at the port in time to meet the boat and he would get the pick of the catch for supper.

He jogged past some young Africans crouched on the roadside, fiddling with their mobile phones.

He nodded to them politely and they watched him curiously as he thundered by in his sweat-soaked T-shirt. The scrub behind them was strewn with colored food wrappers and squashed drink cartons. He kicked a can to the edge of the road. There was so much rubbish on the island now! Bits of blue plastic sheeting were snagged on the thorn bushes, old food boxes were everywhere.

Twenty years ago when he could have run along the island's roads effortlessly, the Optician of Lampedusa would sometimes spot a scared migrant scrambling up the rocks onto his path. They had almost always been alone and would shout to him in English: "Where am I? Am I in Palermo? Have I reached Sicily?"

He shook his head in disbelief. It seemed a long time ago now. The Arab Spring changed everything and they never came on their own anymore. Big boatloads arrived now in a constant stream—whole families; women and children too, poor things. Only a couple of years ago, the newspapers reported that Lampedusa now had more migrants and refugees than inhabitants! The skin on his forehead wrinkled. Best not to think about that too much, really. The TV, the papers; they were saturated with news about migrants; it was all they talked about.

There was something else on the radio the other day about some more migrants drowning off the coast of Sicily. Seven or eight of them, was it?

He broke his stride to let a scrawny cat slink across the road in front of him and watched it hunker down in the thorn bushes. Of course, he had moved here to get away, really. He'd found the '80s in Naples vacuous; mindless political rows, nothing profound. He'd felt his points of reference just slipping away. This small island though had been the perfect place to construct a new and more meaningful life. Impossible not to feel anchored in this natural beauty. The buttery, limestone cliffs with those idyllic sandy beaches at their base and then the harsh wildness of the north of the island that he found so empowering.

There was laughter suddenly and two middle-aged men, laden with binoculars and expensive-looking cameras, appeared from the bank just in front of him. They were speaking Italian but he could hear they were not locals—bird watchers from Milan most likely. Most of the tourists seemed to be from Milan. They were excited and animated and the younger man called to him that they had just spotted some rare breed of wading bird whose name the Optician didn't catch. He turned inland.

Now that the season was over, there were very few tourists around but it had been a quiet summer altogether. The migrants, he thought, were hardly a positive tourist attraction and many vacationers had chosen Sardinia over Lampedusa for their annual break this year. Friends in the hotel and catering trades complained to him about the drop in takings. Thank God that his own business was not reliant on the tourist trade.

At the entrance to the island's graveyard, a gray-haired man in a bright blue polo shirt was hunched over a bench, drilling breeze-blocks. The concrete slabs spat out orange sparks as he worked and the Optician wondered vaguely what he was making so intently. The crosses on top of the beveled mausoleums glinted in the early evening light.

He was on the homeward stretch now and feeling positive. Tomorrow he was awarding himself a couple of days off to take a boat trip with his wife and some close friends. It would be good to switch off for a bit, to stop worrying about the accounts, about the boys' futures, and to just watch the open sea roll out before him, with all her vastness and possibilities. He looked up at the cloudless sky and his thin lips stretched into a grin. Promising weather.

His friend Francesco had spent the morning polishing *Galata*, scrubbing her royal-blue and brick-red hull, sprucing her up for her imminent outing. He smiled indulgently. Good old Francesco! They'd had some laughs on that boat over the years. Francesco treated her as if she were a luxury yacht rather than a tarted-up fifteen meter (fifty foot) wooden fishing boat. He kept the white paint of her wheelhouse immaculate.

There was already a small line at the fishmongers on the harbor front. Laid out on the crushed ice trays he saw bluefin tuna, round-bellied *sardinella*, and huge, long-billed swordfish. A shop worker was helping the last of the fishermen to unload his catch of bruise-colored squid, the purple, jellied tentacles spilling over the side of the box.

It was the last push up the hill and then onto the Via Roma to his little flat above the shop for a shower. On his left, beached in a huge car park, were the jumbled wrecks of wooden boats that had brought migrants to the island from Libya. Tipped awkwardly onto their sides, their cracked hulls were blistered with cheerful turquoise and ox-blood paint.

But the Optician had other things on his mind. Right now, he was hungry and he wanted to shower and to buy some sardines at the portside for supper with his wife. He needed to call his friend Matteo about what supplies to pack for their boating trip and to work out who was bringing the wine. It would be a fun trip with all eight of them out on the water together.

Perhaps, if the wind had suddenly picked up spirit that night as it so often did in Lampedusa and had begun to thrash the little fishing boats against the harbor sea wall and to needle the sea until it raged in fury, the Optician would never have boarded his friend's little pleasure boat and would never have cast off. He would have simply postponed his trip and gone out with his friends for *aperitivi* at the usual bar, then maybe on to dinner at one of the local restaurants. He would have been disappointed—irritated perhaps. In the morning, at his shop when a customer who was choosing new frames for his glasses politely asked him what he had been up to lately, he would have shrugged and replied that frankly, he had nothing to tell.

But the wind stayed soft. And he did cast off.

CHAPTER 2

The door leading to the apartment was open when he arrived back at the shop. He hated that. He hated when the lines between work and private life got blurred. Customers were so nosy when they heard the door creak open and saw Teresa coming downstairs: they always craned their necks to try to see inside the door, to get a glimpse of how the Optician and his wife lived. It irritated him how fascinated people were by his private living arrangements.

He closed the door firmly and jogged up the stairs, where he found Teresa in the sitting room reading a magazine.

"The door was open again," he said pointedly. She smiled vaguely and looked up briefly from her reading.

"Was it, dear?" she asked, playing with the thick strands of her blonde hair. "Oh well."

The sitting room was hot with the day's sunshine and Teresa had left the window wide open. The pages of the novel he'd been reading yesterday fanned a little in the light breeze and he picked up the book and flattened it between his palms, carefully running his thumb down the spine before slotting it back into the weathered wooden bookcase. He'd like to replace the furniture in here one day soon; it was all getting a little tired-looking, especially the glass coffee table which was scored and scratched all over. The strong light accentuated its imperfections; it made him wince to see the damaged glass. The sun had taken the color out of the damask rug; the edge that tucked under the sofa was still slate blue but the rest had faded to an insipid dove gray. The old sofa had perked up a bit after Teresa had taken the covers to the dry cleaners, although he swore that was the last time they would ever buy anything in cream.

He went into the little kitchen, took the glass that was standing on the draining board, and poured himself a large glass of water from the bottle in the fridge. He knocked it back quickly and poured himself another. He wandered back to the doorway of the sitting room. His wife had been right to insist that they get that chap to paint up here as well when they'd redecorated the shop last year. The white walls made the place look cleaner and bigger than it was. Not that there was much furniture in here; thankfully Teresa had the same views as him on unnecessary clutter.

"I thought I'd get sardines for supper," he said, addressing the back of his wife's head. "I saw the boat come in."

Teresa craned her neck to look at him, wrinkling her nose.

"Aren't you going to shower, dear?" she replied.

In the shower, he thought about what he needed to pack for the trip tomorrow. Were his apple-green swimming shorts clean? He'd rather take them than the new navy ones that his youngest son had given him for his birthday. Things got torn on boats. On that last trip they'd taken with Francesco in the summer, he'd ripped his windbreaker on the corner of the table in the cabin; he had mended it carefully, re-stitching the pocket so that you couldn't really tell it had ever been otherwise but the fact was that he knew that it was damaged and it annoyed him to think of it even now. He liked to be careful with his things. He'd pack the new pair of fake Converse that he'd picked up at the Naples market: it wouldn't be a tragedy if they got salt stained. He smiled to himself. They were the same dark gray as his friend Matteo's except his had cost fifteen euros whereas Matteo's had set him back over sixty. He could still see Matteo's stunned face when he'd told him last week. His friend had bent down and examined them, checked the soles, rubbed the cotton tongue between his finger and thumb and cursed. He chuckled as the hot water ran down his back. He enjoyed getting one over on that young upstart! It always felt good to teach the young ones a trick or two. Not that Matteo was exactly a spring chicken anymore; he had already said goodbye to forty but Matteo did love to rib him about his own impending sixtieth birthday. The cheeky bugger even called Francesco "Granddad."

He looked at himself in the mirror as he toweled himself dry. You had to admit he wasn't doing badly for a man in his late fifties. There was no spare flesh on him really and his stomach had resisted developing a middle-aged paunch. He flexed his chest muscles and saw the sinews stretch. It wasn't about vanity, this "keeping fit" business. He just didn't like to let himself go. Discipline. You went nowhere in life without discipline. This was what he'd always told his sons during their early teenage years when they had just wanted to lie around the house with headphones on like zombies. Discipline and damn hard work. That's what you needed if you wanted to get somewhere, he had told his boys while they rolled their eyes at him and pretended to drop off to sleep in boredom. He peered at an age spot on his bald forehead. Mind you, the message had managed to filter into them through those headphones of theirs somehow or other. He was proud of them both. He really was. He loved to talk about them to Gabriele and Francesco, to show them the latest photos. He was careful though not to sound boastful; no one likes a show-off. He grinned in the mirror. He had good teeth.

There was a small canvas bag on the bed. Teresa must have already packed her stuff. He made a mental note to remind her to bring a fleece or a warm sweater; it was bright sunshine now all right but early October could be fickle with its winds. He'd pack in the morning. He was in a hurry to get back down to the port and buy those sardines before someone else snaffled them up. He would never buy them if there was only a scattering left in the tray; he always suspected that the fishmonger bulked them out with a few of yesterday's leftover catch when stocks ran low. Buying fish was very much his job. Teresa never seemed to notice when the sardines looked tired or dry. His wife trusted everyone. Always giving people the benefit of the doubt.

He picked up the white shirt he'd been wearing this morning from the bed and flicked at a bit of grime around the right cuff. The shirt would do for tonight, for frying sardines. He heard the phone ring as he put on his shirt and as soon as he heard his wife's giggles he guessed it was Maria on the other end. Those two together! Thick as thieves. Teresa called to him from the sitting room.

"Maria fancies dinner out tonight," she said, "to mark the start of our holiday. Giulia's coming too and Gabriele—shall we join them?"

He checked his watch. It was touch and go whether he'd even make the fishmongers now. He hesitated. He hated changing plans. Oh well, why not! Teresa would love it and it would be a good way to sort out who was bringing what for the boat trip tomorrow rather than sending round umpteen group texts. Besides, it would give him an hour or so downstairs to make sure everything was in order in the shop before they went away on their little break.

"Fine!" he called through the door. "But not that awful place Matteo chose last week—the electric light in there is offensive!"

He changed out of the white shirt and slipped on the clean black one from the hanger that was hooked onto the back of the bedroom door. It smelled of lavender and vaguely of Teresa. She was fastidious with the ironing, he thought, as he buttoned it up and smoothed down the front.

He stretched at the top of the stairs, touching his hands to the floor and bouncing there for a few moments. He fancied he could hear his spine creaking. He'd have to see about his back one of these days. A stiff back was a hazard of the job. You spent half your day as an Optician twisting over retinoscopes and ophthalmoscopes and the other half was spent crouched at a desk doing the paperwork.

Teresa had filled the jug behind the counter with some big paper sunflowers and he was surprised he hadn't noticed them when he'd walked into the shop after his run. He sized them up suspiciously, wondering if they weren't a little garish. No, on balance Teresa was right. Their bright yellow was clean and cheery and somehow made the shop look less clinical. It may not feel like it now but autumn would creep up quickly on Lampedusa. The sky would turn sour and moldy and then they would need every bit of help they could get to lure people through the doors to shift last season's sunglasses.

THE OPTICIAN OF LAMPEDUSA

He picked up the diary to make sure that Teresa had canceled all his appointments for the next couple of days. He saw she had highlighted a name in pink for next Wednesday. Oh yes. Mrs. Maggiorani. She always needed a courtesy call the night before to remind her she had an appointment.

It was unbelievable really that some people led such muddled lives. He was a list maker. Every day he made a neat list of tasks he had to do and goals he wanted to achieve and every evening he ticked them off. That way you kept track; you kept on top of things. He rubbed out a line in the diary reminding him to chase up the lab for Mr. Esposito's bifocals. He'd done that this morning from his mobile while he was on hold on the landline to a supplier in Naples. You had to show life very clearly who was boss—who was in command—or life would quickly take advantage and wreak havoc.

He leafed through the mail to see if there was anything that Teresa had missed. There was that "thank you" letter from the old lady in Turin she had told him about over lunch. He'd fixed her glasses back in early September when she'd come over for a vacation to see her sister. She'd dropped them off a balcony and was so distraught when she'd come in to see him because she couldn't read without them. It had taken him a couple of days to sort them out and to find the right lens but he'd fixed her up with something else to be getting along with. She had been stunned when he'd said there was no charge. He'd had all the stuff in the shop anyway so it wasn't a problem and she was a nice old dear. Honest, she said about him in her letter. Lovely to meet such an honest man. He smiled to himself. It was not often that you heard a man from Naples being described as honest. That had been one of the reasons he had left actually: he just couldn't bear being tainted with the same overtones of double-dealing and corruption as his home city.

You had to be trustworthy as an Optician. There was an intimacy about his job, about peering right inside someone's eyeballs, your face just inches from theirs. At the beginning of his studies, his father had worried that he might be too shy for such close contact with strangers but he had found it easier to be polite then to distance himself, breaking down the person into retina, blood vessels, and optic nerves. Funnily enough, Teresa often told him nowadays that he had a tendency to stare at people when he was out with them, as if he was examining them. A tic of the job, he supposed—a habit. She'd nudge him under the table when he was doing it; it made people uncomfortable, she said, to feel as if they were under the microscope when they were trying to have dinner.

Right. What else was left to do? He looked over at the display case containing the contact lenses and solutions. No, that was all well stocked. Although—how had that happened—someone had put a green bottle of saline solution on the shelf that was meant for the blue gas permeable products. He rearranged the shelf correctly, frowning.

Teresa came downstairs and handed him his black jacket. Time to go, she said. She was wearing the long silver necklace he liked, the one with the intertwining strands which she fiddled with when she was nervous. Her blonde hair spilled over the shoulders of her silky gray top. It was still as thick and copious as it had been when he'd first met her as a fourteen-year-old schoolgirl.

"Maria has booked the restaurant on the little hill overlooking the port," she said.

He opened his mouth to speak.

"The one you like," she added, firmly taking his arm.

Before he flicked off the light switch, he moved the men's sunglasses stand an inch or two to the right so that it was symmetrical with the women's stand, opposite.

His own street was Lampedusa's commercial hub, a wide pedestrianized boulevard with polished gray flagstones that shone under the electric light of the street lamps. It was the only place on the island suitable for an evening *passeggiata* and was peppered with wooden benches, smart cafes, and boutiques. Lampedusa had never gone in for high-rise: almost all the apartment blocks and shops on the street were only two or three stories high and they were pressed close together in terraces to make the best use of space. Most of the houses' facades were the rich cream color of the local lime plaster. Others had had a modern makeover and sported walls in shades of lemon, sulphur, and mustard. Behind Via Roma, the streets were narrower and shabbier. There was always building work taking place on the island, always some house or apartment standing naked and un-rendered. He'd lost track of which buildings were actually being constructed or renovated and which ones had just been abandoned to crumble into the ground. A neighbor called out good evening to them from her balcony as they headed to the port, peeping over the top of some bedsheets that were drying on her washing line.

The season may have been over, but the restaurant was packed. They were lucky, Maria was saying, to get a table. Her pink lip-gloss felt sticky on his cheek as she kissed him. He sat next to Giulia who as usual was battling to tame her frizz of hair. She was torturing her curls into an elastic band behind her head as she greeted him, swearing as one of those dangly turtle earrings she always wore got caught up and imprisoned. She looked tired, he thought. It was a busy time of year for Giulia and her partner, Gabriele—they were packing up their beach accessories shop for the winter, going through stock that needed to be sold off and sorting items for storage for when they reopened in March. "IF we reopen in March," she muttered. The business rents were soaring so fast you had to be a millionaire to keep up with them. She and the Optician raised their eyebrows at one another and clinked their water glasses together.

"Where is the wine?" Maria asked, looking round for the waiter. Gabriele had ordered the Sicilian red but the Optician was skeptical and had asked for a small glass to taste first. Maria would be closing up her swimsuit boutique for the winter soon and heading back to Catania. He could hear her telling the girls to pop by over the next couple of weeks if they wanted a look in before she put the costumes on general sale. Her neck was draped with a long gold scarf that was knitted like rigging rope. He recognized it as the one Teresa had pointed out to him in her shop window last week. Maria always had on something different. He looked at her fondly. He liked that she took risks with her clothes, that she dared to be maverick. Teresa was much more classic, he thought, as he watched his wife play with the strands of her silver necklace. Teresa pulled off classic beautifully.

He laughed at Gabriele who held the menu far away from his face, peering as he tried to decipher what was written on it. He nudged Maria.

"Admit that you're getting as old as the rest of us!" Maria teased Gabriele. "Go and see our bald friend here and get your beautiful blue eyes fitted with some glasses!"

Gabriele was a serious chap. Teresa always described him as "dependable," and she was right. They were close neighbors and often hooked up for *aperitivi* on a summer's evening when the tourists had gone to dinner. If ever he had to go to Sicily or to Naples on an overnight work trip, Gabriele would be sure to swing by to make sure Teresa was OK on her own.

The red wine was thin and lacked generosity. He ordered the white.

The women were admiring Elena's new hairstyle. She had added a thick streak of blonde to her dark fringe. Less accountant, more Lampedusa, she joked, flicking back her long hair over her shoulder. She clowned a sad face. She was dreading leaving the sunshine and the big wide skies of the island to return to the cramped dull finance office in the north of Italy where she worked during the winter months. She made a grab for the bottle of wine.

Buone vacanze! she gasped, filling her glass to the brim and slurping the wine like a desperate alcoholic. They all laughed.

He and Teresa sat out the *primo piatto;* they were careful not to eat too many carbohydrates in the evening. The waiter brought him the platter of sea bream and swordfish to inspect and he considered them carefully, asking for precise details of exactly where and when they were caught. He listened intently to the waiter's replies, his gaze probing the man's perspiring face. He felt Teresa giving him a warning tug on his jacket. He chose the sea bream. The eyes on the swordfish looked a little milky.

Giulia exchanged a private look with Teresa who giggled surreptitiously behind her sleeve. He looked at them, feigning hurt.

"How does she put up with you?" Giulia mocked. "Mr. Fastidious!" He threw his hands in the air.

Matteo would also soon be heading back to the mainland, Maria told them over the fish (which incidentally was very good—they all had to agree he had made the right choice). It had been a bad year for Matteo workwise, a real struggle to get a job, she was saying. And Francesco had a call from the workshop this morning, she added. He and his carpentry skills were needed back in Milan by the end of the month, much earlier than he would have liked. He'd have to leave his daughter running the ice cream parlor alone for a bit. They all groaned in sympathy. No one liked leaving the island.

He took out his tobacco pouch and began to roll himself a cigarette. One after a meal was the limit. Just the one. He excused himself from the table.

There was still no sign of a wind outside and the air, although warm, was losing its sweet scent of summer. He could hear the gentle clinking of the boats as the sea teased them away from their chains and he knew that somewhere out there in the dark, *Galata* was waiting for them. He'd have a look at the maritime forecast when he got home. He knew that Francesco would have already checked but he'd have a look anyway. A wind this warm and light could mean the treacherous sirocco was on its way. It blew in stealthily from the Sahara, picking up speed across Libya, roaring its way over the Mediterranean until it burst open on Sicily and Lampedusa. And when the sirocco came, that's when you knew autumn was on its way too, prompting half the islanders to pack up, turn around, and sit out the winter on the mainland.

He extinguished his cigarette. It was a funny time of year, October. The beginning of the end, really.

CHAPTER 3

The Optician of Lampedusa stretched out lazily in his bunk and felt the first tentative shafts of early morning light play across his face, teasing him out of slumber. The swell underneath the boat rocked him gently into consciousness and into the delicious realization that he was on vacation and that today no one was going to badger him about broken frames or complain about scratched lenses. He sighed contentedly. Such peace. Everyone else on board was still asleep. As he set the water boiling for his coffee, he could already hear the first seagulls squabbling.

Up on the deck, feeling a little chilly in the dawn dampness, the Optician clutched his coffee cup and zipped up the collar of his navy windbreaker as he watched the fledgling sunrise. The wind was light: it was barely tickling the water. The sun, as it rose higher and hotter, would have no problem pushing away the few light clouds that were currently pestering the new sky. It looked to be a glorious morning for a pleasure cruise and a spot of fishing. A ripple of childish excitement pulsed through him. How he loved the sea! The immensity of it! He'd always found being on the water so restorative and being with his close friends out here—well, that was about as good as it got.

They'd had a laugh last night. Old Francesco was such a good raconteur after a glass or two, his gray ponytail stiff with salt, looking like a sea-soned country and western star as he told his tall tales. Matteo egged him on like nothing else. Poor Gabriele had copped it all day. Mind you, he was happy not to be the butt of all the jokes himself: they were always teasing him about being so finicky and precise, wanting everything done just so in a very particular way.

He grinned. Gabriele fancied himself quite the fisherman yet he'd been the only one of the boys not to contribute a single fish to the supper pail. They'd watched him getting more and more irritated as fish were landed and dropped in the bucket. Time and time again he'd reeled in his line, checked the bait, found nothing, sighed huffily, and recast.

He had no idea, his rod being on the other side of the boat, that Matteo was teasing him by repeatedly slapping the same fish into the bucket. Matteo's supposed good fortune had driven Gabriele's competitive spirit into overdrive; Maria and Teresa were doubled up, clutching each other, biting their lips to stop the sound of their laughter giving the game away.

It had been great to see Teresa let herself go like that. She was such a worrier. But she always relaxed around Maria—everyone did really. You'd never met a warmer woman; she was always clucking round, making sure that everyone was happy and feeling included without ever overstepping the mark into irritating do-gooder territory. He smiled indulgently. What a great softie she was! It was Maria who'd called out the prank on Gabriele; she couldn't bear to see him made a fool of.

Gabriele had gone nuts. He'd leapt on top of Matteo, knocking him to the floor, trying to slap his bearded face with the fish and then tussling and struggling with him on the deck until they'd both slid off the stern steps and had plummeted into the sea. Giulia had filmed some of it on her smartphone camera. When they'd watched the video later, the images had been about as smooth as if she'd filmed in a force nine hurricane—she'd been laughing so much that she couldn't hold the phone still.

They'd all ended up in the sea afterward. One by one, they'd dived in, whooping like children, splashing each other, chasing the last light of the evening before the sun sank and its fiery colors fizzled out as it hit the waterline. The autumn chill had yet to spoil the water; it was still twenty-one degrees Celsius. Mucking around with his friends, the Optician could still sense the optimism of summer. What was it Elena had said when she was floating beside him, her long dark hair fanning out around her head? That swimming in the autumn was like a rebirth. If you got a few good swims behind you in October you felt renewed and ready to face the winter ahead.

He'd stayed in for a little while after the others had climbed out and were hosing themselves down on the steps. It was wonderful to be in the darkening velvety warmth of the sea, letting the swell take his body and push and nudge it wherever it pleased, its rhythmic music accompanied by the tinkling laughter of his friends.

It had been so deliciously peaceful and welcoming. He'd almost felt guilty when he'd started swimming. It seemed barbaric somehow to churn up this glassy water with all that kicking and chopping. So he'd stroked through it very gently, barely troubling the surface like a polite and courteous guest tiptoeing through a house at night so as not to disturb his host.

Yes, he was grateful to the sea all right. Its salt was still tight on his skin from yesterday's swim. It changed your ideas, the sea did. Made you see things more clearly, more positively somehow. All this calm. Although, he thought with a tiny pang of annoyance, it would be even better if those seagulls would tone it down a bit.

His coffee was almost cold now. He drained the cup and wondered whether he should fetch another or enjoy the last few moments of solitude before the others came up on deck. He could already feel someone stirring in the cabin below. He stretched and rolled his head slowly in a circle, listening to his neck crack. He deserved this vacation and he wanted to savor every little golden moment of it.

But something was niggling at him. There was something about the way the seagulls were mewling that had him on edge. It was the pitch of the damned birds. They were never satisfied, always complaining or bickering and picking petty squabbles with each other. His skin prickled with irritation.

Matteo came up on deck, shirtless, his arms and chest crisscrossed with a dark pattern of intertwined tattoos. His finger was in the air. He didn't pause to wish his friend good morning. He was concentrating on listening to something.

"Do you hear it?" Matteo asked the Optician urgently. "There's something out there."

The Optician strained his ears to the sound. "It's not seagulls?" he asked. "Seagulls screaming?"

Gabriele and Francesco joined them. "Something is screaming," Gabriele confirmed slowly, "but I don't think it's seagulls, do you Francesco?"

Francesco held the cold, metal gunwale of his boat and listened. This sound didn't make sense.

The men stood silent for a long moment and peered across the water at the cat's paw prints on the springy surface. As the women hurried from their bunks and rocked the cabin below, a few small waves slapped the boat's hull and the mewling noise was gone for a few seconds. The sea calmed itself but almost immediately the wind threw back the eerie sound again, a sort of animalistic baying. The Optician shuddered involuntarily.

"What is it?" he whispered. "What's out there?"

His eyes darted nervously around the boat. There were no lights out on the dark water, no other vessels. Aside from the sinister intermittent shrieking they were on their own.

But Francesco had already started the engine.

As the men pulled up the anchor, the women scrambled up onto the deck.

"What's going on? What's that awful noise?"

His wife Teresa sounded panicky—she was easily flustered and upset by sudden problems. She was fifty now, but she'd never really shrugged off her childish sense of innocence and wonder. It made her very endearing; practically everyone she had ever met had wanted to protect her. But the Optician often worried that her openness also left her vulnerable. He sometimes told her she needed to toughen up.

"We're sorting it out," he promised her as soothingly as he could. "We're going to take a look. Yell if you see something, girls."

"But it sounds like something is really suffering," she insisted. "It sounds like something is in pain." She held the edge of his windbreaker and looked up at him anxiously.

"We're sorting it out," the Optician replied firmly.

Teresa, Maria, and Elena took up posts at the bow. Freed of her anchor, *Galata* chugged out of the mouth of the protected cove and into the open sea. Waves struck the boat's hull with greater force and the Optician checked his watch mechanically—it was just after six o'clock. He swung himself up onto the roof of the cabin to get a clearer view of the water. The sea dutifully reflected back the orange sky. Whatever was out there was giving no clues.

Matteo and Gabriele paced the little boat, swearing under their breath impatiently. The women were silent at their posts, breathing heavily, afraid. The Optician's wife gripped Elena's arm.

The motorboat's outboard engine sliced easily through the water, leaving behind a trail of frothing backwash that split into two like a whale's fin. Yesterday afternoon the Optician had sat at the stern for a good half an hour, transfixed by the hypnotic regularity of the wake, his mind lulled and comforted by the continually splitting vortex. Now he watched the disturbed water nervously as his finger worried at the pulsating vein on his right temple.

"See anything?" Matteo shouted up to him.

He shook his head and the two men exchanged looks of bafflement.

Now he couldn't hear the damned noise anymore at all. Were they even on the right course? He whistled to Gabriele and when he looked up, he tapped both his ears in an exaggerated mime of deafness. Gabriele yelled down to Francesco to cut the engine and its throaty roar petered out and died.

Galata shuddered spasmodically in the water from the brutal braking, lurching and trembling. Her crew, motionless, waited for the sea to settle. Maria leaned over and took Teresa's other arm. Giulia, standing a little apart from the others, was biting the knuckles of her right hand, her left hand struggling to pull back her rebellious hair. How vulnerable they looked, the four of them. He was alarmed for them but he knew he must not show it.

This time, the monstrous, tortured howl ripped through everyone like a bullet. Instinctively, the Optician moved his hand to protect his face.

He staggered to keep his footing on the cabin roof. What the hell was out there?

The howl mutated into an unbearable screeching. The Optician felt his stomach knot. Something was roaring underneath the waves. Whatever it was, the Optician had a gut feeling that when they found it, it would be truly terrible. He forced himself to regulate his breathing and tried to nod reassuringly at Teresa who was looking at him in horror.

Then, suddenly he saw something.

"Fish! I see three big fish there! Francesco—five o'clock!"

Francesco maneuvered the boat in the direction of his outstretched arm. The Optician kept his eye trained on the black dots he saw bobbing on the water and tried to steady his mind. But his brain was arguing with his eyes. What kind of fish would be on the surface of the water, idiot? Come on, what kind of fish?

"More fish there!" Maria was pointing slightly to the right of his outstretched arm, leaning over the rail, her face screwed up to the sun. But the Optician was still staring with a professional intensity at the objects he had spotted, focused as fixedly as a customer in his own shop sitting in front of the reading charts. He willed his eyes and brain to recognize and interpret the forms.

Galata drifted closer, the little boat dancing nervously up and down in the slight swell. They were thirty meters away and the frenetic clamoring was intensifying.

The Optician recoiled. One of the black shapes he was watching lengthened, partly lifting up from the water and then flopping down again into a ball. It disappeared, leaving a white froth of disturbed water.

Oh God no. Please God no.

"People!" Giulia screamed. "There are people in the water!"

Standing high above the water level on the cabin roof, his arm still outstretched, the Optician saw the black dots come into focus. Bodies were flung like bowling pins across the sea's glassy surface, some bobbing precariously, some horizontal and horribly heavy. The people in the water had all seen *Galata* now and they were churning the sea into a frenzy with their flailing arms and legs. Every time a wave collapsed, another black dot or head was revealed. The sea was littered with them.

The ocean reverberated with their screaming, the terrible sound bouncing off of and coming from under the water, gargling and rupturing. The Optician recognized the screams as the music of the dying, the final dirges of the drowning. In the chorus of voices he could pick out each individual soloist. Everyone was begging to be noticed.

The Optician swallowed.

How, he thought, do I save them all?

He lowered his outstretched arm slowly. In the water, hands snatched despairingly upward, clutching at air, reaching futilely toward him.

He could see yellowing eyes staring wide and wild at him, frantic with the hope of salvation.

He glanced down at his friends on deck. Eight. There were eight of them and there were hundreds of people in the water. And they had just one life preserver.

Even before he jumped down from the cabin and onto the deck, the Optician had understood that they would have to choose who would live and who would die.

CHAPTER 4

There had been no arguments about who should give orders, not a second wasted in debate over who should perform what function or who should stand where. Matteo, without hesitating, simply dived into the water and started dragging people toward the boat. Gabriele raced into the cockpit and gave the mayday emergency call on the radio.

The Optician was sweating even before Matteo had hauled the first spluttering man to the boat's stern. He ripped off his windbreaker and he could feel the blood pumping through his chest and limbs, his body gushing adrenaline as he stood on the wooden deck. His muscles itched to be used and his breathing was impatient.

The first person they pulled from the sea looked barely more than a boy. The Optician and Francesco had hauled him up by his wrists but the young chap was completely naked, covered in diesel and as slippery as a fish. He slipped back under. When he resurfaced again spluttering and crying, it was been difficult to find purchase on his oily flesh, which was as smooth and polished as an aubergine. The Optician's nails bit into the dark skin as he yanked him aboard. He'd never held anyone's hand so tightly before—the intimacy of the gesture with a naked total stranger made him wince. Yet when the force of the pull had flung the man up against his bare chest, he'd felt something strangely primeval stir in him, something almost like love. He'd wanted to hold the adolescent, to hug him in the same way he had done with his own sons when they were frightened or in trouble.

But there wasn't time for emotion. Matteo was already yelling for help with the next survivor and was struggling to free himself from him; his head was being intermittently forced underwater as the drowning man clutched at his neck and scrabbled with his feet, trying to hook his legs around Matteo's tattooed torso. All around the boat, from every direction, voices shrieked in panic.

"You'll be fine, you'll be fine!" the Optician shouted to the young man over his shoulder. "We're going to save your friends now—don't worry!"

On the deck, the teenager had instantly rolled into a fetal ball, vomiting seawater and shaking so hard the women thought he might be having a seizure. He was weeping and moaning to himself in a language that they didn't understand.

He screamed when Maria touched his shoulder, pulling backward, covering his private parts with his trembling hands. Sensitive Teresa understood his shame immediately and dashed below the deck to get her weekend bag. The first thing she pulled from the canvas was a vermillion T-shirt and he snatched it from her to hide himself. He put his legs through the armholes and wore the T-shirt like a giant pair of underpants or a diaper, knotting the material at the side. He sobbed like a baby, rocking.

There was a question that needed to be asked, although the Optician was not sure he was ready for the answer. He steeled himself.

"How many of you were on the boat?" he asked, counting on his fingers to indicate numbers. The exhausted teenager leaned forward and with his finger, traced a figure on the deck. Five hundred. The Optician's mouth fell open. The young man leaned forward again and added a symbol. Plus.

Three men were now on board and Gabriele maneuvered the boat toward the next little group.

Everyone seemed to understand implicitly to focus their rescue efforts on the clusters of survivors rather than on lone individuals; no one protested when they let a corpse smack back down under the quartzy surface. In addition to Gabriele's distress call, the girls had telephoned the emergency services from Elena's mobile but there was no sign of backup yet. It was fully light now and the Optician could make out dots over a five-hundred-meter radius.

"Propeller!" he screamed. "We need to go slower! We're going to slice them up with the bloody propeller!"

Galata zigzagged through the small waves, picking her way through the debris of corpses and the discarded clothing and shoes. It felt so ugly, thought the Optician, not to stop and retrieve the dead, but they didn't matter now, not while there were others out there who still had life in them, who still had a chance.

The next two men they dragged from the sea were so close to death that the Optician feared they'd die on board. Saltwater and shock had wrecked their intestines and they were retching and defecating all over the deck. Their eyelids fluttered as they drifted in and out of consciousness. Their bodies were exhausted with the struggle and their spirits were only just flickering. Teresa and Maria tucked sleeping bags from the bunks around their shuddering forms, willing them to stay alive.

"Thirty meters away—7 o'clock!" yelled Francesco.

There were four men in the next huddle, all clinging to each other, splayed out in an ungainly formation, splashing the water with their forearms as they tried to stay afloat. In the clear water, the soles of their feet flashed pink as they kicked upward, thrashing like fish in a net. Kneeling with his arm outstretched, the Optician waited for their fists to close on his.

He would never forget the feel of all those slippery wet hands. Power rippled through the sinews of his back as he willed survivors from the water. He had never felt so alive in his whole life—he could feel vitality sparking, flaring, flashing through his nerves and muscles. He needed to make these dots in the water feel it, too. He felt he had the energy to reanimate them all if only he could reach them in time. His friends' zeal was electrifying and spurred him forward.

"Come on guys, we need to move faster!"

One of the men they'd rescued was hysterical, jabbing his finger at the water, holding on to the

Optician. He kept repeating a word over and over again but he didn't seem to understand any Italian.

It was Matteo who thought to try to speak in English.

"What do you want?" he asked. "We can help if you tell us slowly in English."

The man looked at them all imploringly, tears pouring down his face.

"Please," he said, holding his hands together as if in prayer. "Children. There are many children."

Francesco jumped in the water then too, kicking downward, his eyes stinging in the saltwater. He exploded back onto the surface of the water after a minute or so and then raced back to the boat like a man chased by a shark. The Optician did not need an explanation and nor did any of the others—they all knew from the shock on Francesco's face that under the waves he'd been nudged and bumped by the blunt, clumsy forms of corpses.

The Optician found himself praying silently to a God he didn't believe in. Just save the children. Please let us find the children. Whatever happens, for God's sake, let me help the children.

But they never found any children.

"Let's move on!" said Francesco determinedly and Gabriele thrust the engine forward.

By the time they reached the trio of people that Maria had spotted, there were only two heads left above the water level.

"It's a woman!" Maria leaned over the side of the boat as Gabriele steered it tentatively toward the group. "There's a man too, but I'm sure there's a woman!"

Francesco threw the life preserver to the woman but it was the man who caught it. The Optician watched as the man pulled it toward her but she seemed disinterested and wouldn't grab it despite his frantic cajoling. Her left hand lay across the bobbing back of the dead man beside her and her long braids were splayed out in the water as her head drooped sideways; it was clear she was giving up and was going the same way as the corpse she was clinging to. The man in the water beside her tried to pry her hands loose and put them on the life preserver, pleading with her to let the dead man go.

The Optician knew it was futile to plead in Italian, but he did it all the same. Teresa and Maria cried out to her to come with them, reassuring her that it would soon all be over. At the sound of the female voices, the young woman opened her eyes, raised her chin slightly, and looked up at them.

With the last drop of her strength, she lifted her arm and flopped it onto the ring. She was wearing a turquoise T-shirt slicked with oil, and nothing else.

It was almost as if she hadn't wanted to be saved, the Optician thought. She slithered onto the deck in a pool of diesel and seawater like a fish with the struggle gone out of it. When he put his hand to her cheek, she cowered, her hands pulling down at the hem of her T-shirt, trying to hide her nudity and her humiliation. He wanted desperately to reassure her but her fear of him, and of Francesco and Matteo, was tangible; he could feel that they were hurting her just by looking at her. Yet when Teresa laid a beach towel over her body, she sat up instantly and touched Teresa's hand.

"Thank you," she whispered in English in a cracked voice and wrapped the towel around her waist. As they tried to comfort this tiny woman, Teresa and Maria wept openly. The young woman remained impassive. She sat with her chin slightly upward, looking almost haughty as she choked back her grief. Was she too proud to weep or just too broken? In their own sparse English and with much sign language they showered her with questions: did she want water, did she want to take off the wet turquoise T-shirt and put on the dry sweatshirt they offered, was the dead man she clung to her husband, were there any other women on board?

She turned her head to the sea where the corpse was still visible, floating crudely, face downward in the swell. She stared at the form for a long moment before turning her back.

"He was my brother," she said quietly and without self-pity. "And yes, there were many women."

She did not speak again and although they all checked on her frequently, none of them once saw her cry. Nor did they find any other women.

After they'd exhausted the first search area, Gabriele took control of the boat, while the Optician and Francesco yanked and dragged the people on board. The women had been incredible, taking it in turns to scour the sea, to nurse, and to comfort. Their teamwork was a factory conveyor belt, saving, sorting, securing. Afterward, the Optician thought it was as if they had been purposefully selected for this task—as if all their lives, they'd been subconsciously practicing for this day.

CHAPTER 5

Everywhere he looked, there were more of them. They seemed to multiply in the water, hands breeding hands. The Optician looked at his watch and felt panic rise up in his throat—he knew they were working against the clock here. Where the hell was the Coast Guard? All this time he was taunted by the nagging doubt that they weren't doing this right; that a professional crew would do things differently, more efficiently, would be saving more people. If only they could work faster!

The women had practically ripped the boat to pieces: when they'd exhausted all the clothes from everyone's bags and rucksacks, they'd torn down the curtains from the cabin windows. Even the rough fabric of the banquettes had been unzipped and yanked off to be used as clothes to try to give the survivors some dignity. Some men had been so mortified to stand before women naked that they'd tried to hurl themselves back into the water.

They'd thrown the buoy to a solitary man whom the Optician had spotted waving to them frantically, but they'd all agreed stoically that they had to plough on toward a group of five people some fifty meters away who were clawing and clutching at each other's bodies. He tried to keep eye contact with the man while they were rescuing the others, calling out to him constantly, promising him they were coming back for him, that he would be saved. But by the time they'd returned, the man had peeled away from the ring and the sea had taken him. No one had spoken when the Optician fished the empty lifebuoy back on board. It felt mockingly light.

Two fishing boats, responding to the mayday call, arrived shortly afterward. Gabriele honked the horn and *Galata*'s crew and the rescued migrants had all yelled at the skippers to slow down because there were afraid the propellers would shred the people still in the water. The Optician saw the fishing boats hesitate—from that distance they could only see a boatload of black people—there were strict laws about aiding illegal immigrants and they were afraid to intervene. He felt fury surge up in him again. How could it be possible that Italy put the law above human lives? He looked at the jumble of wretched survivors crouched on the deck, patched in seat covers, wearing his own old T-shirts and shorts, sobbing for their dead, for their lost women and children. The deck was awash with their vomit, with their tears and feces.

He was tired now but he would not admit it. He'd almost slipped off the stern step during the last rescue: it had felt like his arms were stuffed with cotton wool rather than muscles when he'd tugged the writhing body on board and thumped it down onto the deck. His legs were quivering. But he had to ignore his body's complaints. He had to keep saving lives. There were still people in the water and they needed him.

He had no idea how many they'd rescued now but the boat was bloated. The stern step was almost level with the water line. It was clear they were too low in the water. *Galata* was becoming capricious under the strain and was no longer responding obediently to Gabriele's commands. Her buoyancy was compromised, she was becoming sluggish and dangerously out of control. But there were still people in the water.

Off portside, they could see one of the fishing boats had begun to pluck out the corpses that were littered across the sea. Bodies, swollen with seawater, were slapped down rudely and heavily one by one like cuts of meat on the deck of the boat. Somebody's wife, somebody's brother, somebody's son.

The Optician clambered back up onto the cabin roof to his original viewpoint and began furiously scouring the sea for anything giving off a sign of life. He needed to feel the grasp of another hand, he needed to feel more fingers lock into his, more bone grinding on bone. He was shaking with nervous energy.

"There! Two people! At three o'clock!"

Galata cut drunkenly and unsteadily through the little waves as Gabriele forced the little boat to turn against. Her fenders smacked and bounced across the surface, kicking up spray as the Optician scrambled down onto the deck. Matteo was already on his stomach, hanging over the step, ready to throw the life preserver to the thrashing hands. Come on! Come on! The heads were going under; only the hands, now clenched into fists, were visible. Don't you die! Don't you dare die!

They tore men from the water. They grabbed at hands and yanked the hair on their submerged heads until the faces of the drowning men, eyes rolling with pain, breached the surface. The

Optician felt fingers solder onto his, and he felt the electric rush of power as his body welded with another body. Fueled with adrenaline, Francesco and Matteo almost tossed the first spluttering man on board. The same untamed energy raced through his own veins and he roared as Matteo helped him pitch the second man onto the deck.

Gabriele was shouting now from the wheel-house that he could no longer control the boat. The Optician could feel her straining under the weight of them as she slipped lower in the water. Without warning, panic flooded his stomach. How long could *Galata* hold them up? He watched Teresa stroke a man's forehead as he tried to sip water from a bottle, her small frame supporting the weight of his lolling neck. The boys would never forgive him if he put their mother's life in danger. They would never, ever forgive him. But there were still people in the water!

Two short blasts from the Coast Guard's horn came just as Gabriele was yelling that they needed to start chucking water and stuff from the cabin overboard to lighten the load. At the sound of the horn, the survivors moved as a single herd to the starboard. Unbalanced by the sudden movement, the boat began to tilt and loll, tilt and loll. The migrants screamed in panic.

"Get back! Get back over here! Quickly!" screamed the Optician.

Back up on the cabin roof, the Optician fell onto his knees, clinging to the little barrier with his right arm while waving frantically at the men with his left, screaming at them to move back. Matteo and Francesco lost their footing as the boat swayed violently; they were shouting and pushing the men to the other side of the boat.

"Move! We'll tip over! Move!"

Galata shuddered dangerously before sagging back into the water, belching, overloaded.

Shaking, the Optician got to his feet again and watched the red and white Coast Guard ship approach. There was a little orange Zodiac alongside. He had no idea how many people were on board *Galata* now but he knew it was too many. From his vantage point he did a rapid head count. One, two, three, ten . . . twenty . . . thirty-five . . . forty-six. Forty-six men and one woman. Plus eight crew. That meant there were fifty-five of them. Fifty-five people on a boat built for a maximum of ten.

Underneath him, he could hear the crackles of the VHF radio as Gabriele talked to the approaching Coast Guard. He felt relief that the professionals were coming, that they would soon transfer the migrants they'd rescued to the Coast Guard's boat so Galata could continue the search for survivors without putting anyone's life at risk. He heard Gabriele raise his voice.

Did something just move out there? His eyes probed the sea. Was there someone else there? He blinked and tried to focus as the big blue expanse stared back at him.

Gabriele was shouting from the wheelhouse across to the Coast Guard ship that was now alongside *Galata*'s hull.

"No! You have to take them! We need to keep looking—there are still people in the water!"

The Optician glanced down and saw a Coast Guard officer repeatedly crossing and uncrossing his wrists in a gesture that clearly meant "stop." Surely the officer wasn't telling them they had to give up the search? No, he couldn't be. It would be unthinkable to stop! It would be madness! Was that a hand just there, under the lip of that curled wave or just a shadow? Focus, man!

The Coast Guard's Zodiac had already peeled away and was exploring the water near one of the fishing boats. Come on, come on! He was itching to follow them. They'd be even more efficient now with the professional teams here telling them what to do.

It would be good to follow orders; under their tute-lage, they'd save more people, more quickly. The men on the deck were looking up at him expect-antly. It would be OK. They'd find these survivors' friends and their families. They'd do it.

He glanced down at his wife. It might be best though if Teresa went with the migrants on the Coast Guard's boat. She'd been so tough out here. Really, she'd been incredible, looking out for everyone, thinking on her feet, never stopping for a second. But obviously it was the men who had to carry on with the search. Had to.

The sea pitched and rolled in front of him. Had it been a hand? Had he missed it? His eyeballs throbbed with the effort of concentration. He had to stay focused.

Elena and Maria had now joined in the heated discussion with the Coast Guard's captain and Matteo was arguing furiously.

"Just take some of the passengers! We can carry on here! Don't be ridiculous!"

Francesco was swearing.

The Optician felt his heart pounding. They were being told to abandon the search! They were really being told to give up! It was crazy! This was pure madness—they couldn't give up! They couldn't give up on these people now. They'd saved forty-seven people, damn it! They just needed some help to offload the survivors! For pity's sake, it was unthinkable to slow down the rescue, to give up on these poor people who were counting on them to find the others. Come on!

"Hey!" he shouted down to the Coast Guard aggressively. "There are women and children in the water! We've got to find them and we're wasting time! For God's sake, we don't have time!"

The captain stood firm. It was too dangerous, he insisted, to attempt a transfer of passengers at sea. Anyway, protocol forbade such a move. What they were proposing was against official procedure because it could further endanger lives. It was also clear, insisted the captain, that *Galata*'s crew was exhausted after hours of searching and needed to stop. The Coast Guard, he continued coolly, would take *Galata*'s place alongside the fishing boats. *Galata* must return to Lampedusa's port immediately with the migrant survivors, who would then be taken to the reception center for medical attention. He crossed his arms to make an *X* shape. Other boats were now on hand and the time had come to stop.

It was over.

An officer on the Coast Guard ship took a photograph of *Galata* that day at the moment that the captain was giving his orders. She'd sunk so low in the water that one of her fenders was half submerged and a migrant, sitting in the Optician's apple-green swimming shorts with his legs dangling through the safety rail, let his feet drag on the surface. The picture was a little blurry but you could make out Gabriele leaning out of the wheelhouse, his high forehead wrinkled as he strained to hear what was being said by the Coast Guard. A migrant man, perhaps the man most freshly plucked from the sea, peeped out from behind a white bedsheet.

On the roof of the wheelhouse, the Optician, wearing rolled up royal-blue trousers, had his strong bare back to the camera. He was caught in mid-spin, standing with his weight on his right leg, his left leg about to swing round. His gaze was fixed firmly ahead on the huge expanse of water before him and his left arm was poised as if he was about to shout: "There! Two hands at nine o'clock!"

You could see very clearly that it wasn't over for the Optician. Wired by adrenaline, he was still searching, still scouring, still desperate to save.

CHAPTER 6

They cut a pathetic sight as they headed slowly back to port, *Galata* moving sulkily through the water, groaning under her heavy load and protesting each time the sea, bullied by the rising wind, made her path choppier and more difficult. Inside, she had been ravaged: her curtains torn, her cabin shredded; outside, her deck was covered in filth, her motley, ragged crew slumped against her gunwale in abject grief. Almost everyone was crying. The original shrieks of terror had been replaced by a doleful sobbing that made the Optician ache.

At the bow, sitting apart from everyone else, was the only woman they had managed to rescue, her eyes fixed firmly on the approaching land, on the shores of Europe that the Optician imagined she must have longed for with such hope. Her grief was impenetrable, way deeper, he suspected as he scanned her face, than the open sea where her brother and compatriots had just sunk to their deaths. Her suffering seemed so vast and intensely private that he felt almost fearful as he watched her.

Almost no one spoke. Teresa, weeping with the men, held their hands and patted their shoulders, offering water and biscuits silently, mothering and comforting them. He knew he should go to her and take her hand in his, but he did not trust himself to stay strong in her embrace. He was exhausted now, he could feel his body running on empty. But more than his physical fatigue, he felt acutely that something fundamental inside him had fractured. Something was gone from him, had been lifted out of him and lost.

He looked down toward the glittering water. He'd always respected the sea; always known it was far bigger and more powerful than he was. Yet he always felt a sense of kinship whenever he looked out at its sparkling surface. Now he sensed its hostility—or at least its ambiguity—knowing how stealthily and purposefully it had sucked down so many lives into its depths. How many more migrant boats were secretly beached on its bottom? How many more desperate people had given their last breath to the mighty waves? He cast an eye over the men they'd rescued, the men who had cheated the sea. The sea was just teasing them, just letting them think they'd won. In the rippling backwash, he could almost hear the sea laughing, taunting him about those he'd left behind in its grasp.

They had to go back! They just had to! They would drop the survivors at the port and they'd turn around again. He felt the familiar nervous energy trickle into his veins. Of course Gabriele would agree. And he could always count on Francesco and Matteo. They'd go back.

The Optician was shocked by the numbers of police and officials in uniform at the port. They swarmed all over the quayside, radioing, pacing up and down and crowding out curious bystanders. As they docked, some of the migrants cowered at the sight of their guns and truncheons and pulled away from the harsh sound of the sirens of the police vans. He became angry again, wanting to warn the police to back off and he saw similar feelings in his friends' faces. For God's sake, stop treating them like criminals! You have no damn idea what these people have just been through! Teresa pushed forward to *Galata*'s bow, protecting her charges with her own body like an animal might do.

She went to pieces when the men were helped off the boat and put into the police vans. She crumpled onto her knees on the quayside and howled like a mother separated from her children. They had to pry her away from the first man they'd rescued, the teenager to whom she had given her vermillion T-shirt. She clung to his hand with both of hers and when the police officer separated them, she had become hysterical with grief. Maria was the same—Francesco sat down on the pavement with her until she stopped shaking. Elena and Giulia sobbed uncontrollably in each other's arms. They didn't even look up when the police vans started their engines. The Optician wished he hadn't either. He saw the frightened faces stare back at him through the windows, fingers pressed on the glass expectantly and he was overwhelmed with a sense of guilt that he hadn't saved more of them.

He felt helpless. He had no common language with which he could reassure these desperate people and even if he did, he thought bitterly, what could he tell them? That it would be OK and that they would all live happily ever after? He had no idea what the procedure was; he had no clue what was about to happen to them now.

"Some of them are very ill!" he shouted through the open window of the police van. "They need medical help! Please—they've been in the water for hours."

The officer gave him the thumbs-up sign and his electric window slid silently shut. The van pulled off.

Matteo and Gabriele were back on the boat already sluicing down the fouled deck with the hose. Francesco was talking to a police officer, giving him an official statement of what had happened. As the Optician approached them, he heard Francesco say that the sea was "thick with bodies." The Optician interrupted politely and asked the officer if they could give their statements a little later, perhaps that afternoon or in the evening. They'd like, he explained, to rejoin the rescue operation.

The policeman, a heavy man with a weather-worn face, looked at him, puzzled.

"Mate," he said not unkindly. "We've got six boats out there looking now. But it's been hours. There isn't a rescue mission anymore—it's a recovery operation. We've just called in the dive squad."

So it really was over.

The women walked home slowly together—the Optician and the other men stayed to clean *Galata*. They worked quietly and efficiently, saying little to one another as they scrubbed the salty stains from the boat's keel, tidying away ropes and bagging rubbish. The Optician had the impression that they were all overly deliberate with their tasks: none of them seemed in any hurry to call it a day. When they eventually parted at the foot of the little hill leading to the town, they hugged hard like brothers.

Teresa was still sobbing when he came in. She told him she couldn't stop. That she didn't know how to stop. He held her in his arms and felt her slim, fragile body shudder against his. But he found that he just didn't know what to say. He didn't know how to comfort her. He couldn't even make sense of the day's narrative himself. He could find no interpretation of the events that would soften the impact.

As he cuddled his wife, he could still feel the cold, oily skin of that first young man they had plucked from the water—he remembered the boy's heart thumping against his own bare chest, remembered his own visceral joy at feeling the life in him.

He cried a little in the shower. It felt wrong to be comforting himself under this hot water, to be washing away the sweat and tears of this terrible day. He kept thinking of the children they were sup-posed to find, kept thinking how frightened they must have been as the seawater started to pour into their boat. No, he mustn't think of that. Then again, what if there were still people out there, people who were lost and overlooked by the fishing boats and the Coast Guard? What if they were waiting for him?

He had always been a man who had been con-fident about where he was going, a man sure of himself and his decisions. Now he felt that same unnerving splintered feeling he'd sensed on the sad journey back to port. It was as if he'd left a part of himself back in the waves with those people he had not been able to save. Some part of him had died with them.

Had he given all he could? His brain started racing, his memory resurfacing in filmy layers of detail about all the other shipwrecks he knew had already occurred off Lampedusa's coast. He remembered switching off the radio last week when they'd talked about migrants drowning off the coast of Sicily. He had turned away from them. He had not wanted to see their waving hands while he was eating his breakfast. Yet what if he had been there? Perhaps he could have locked his fingers onto their hands and pulled.

He lifted his face to the showerhead and let the water drum over his closed eyes and mouth. His father had always told him that in each of us there is a thick black line above and below which we can measure ourselves and our behavior and against which we can evaluate what is right and what is wrong. He had always felt that black line strongly in himself and had calculated his actions, calculated his priorities and his values accordingly against it. He knew when he'd fallen below the mark. His internal meter warned him when he was about to make a mistake. He checked his life against that bar. And now the line didn't seem straight or constant. It was wavy and intermittent and he could no longer see his position in relation to it. The certainty was gone. He let the hot water pound on his throat and chest but found no solace in it. He felt vulnerable.

He went to work that very afternoon. Immersing himself in work, in the usual routines, was the only way he might hope to get his thoughts tidied up and filed away neatly again, to glue back together his fragmented sense of order. Teresa passed out from nervous exhaustion on the bed and he found something to eat in the fridge and went downstairs to open the shop. He spent a couple of hours going over his stock lists. He called a supplier in

Naples and repaired the sunglasses of some elderly German tourists who had come to the island on a bird-watching vacation.

He behaved professionally, smiling politely, though the entire time he had a scathing sense of how absurd it all was. He now understood the pathetic unimportance of his routines and the insignificance of his work when compared with this morning. At least then he had really known he was alive. This morning had actually mattered.

Unconsciously, he let his hands ball into fists and the aching muscles in his arms tensed, ready to take the strain. He saw the yellow eyes full of terror, the shivering naked bodies slick with the slime of diesel oil, the trembling forms cowering under gaudy beach towels. He realized that he was aching to be back with them. He wanted to take their hands again, to talk to them. He wanted to sit down with them, to ask how they were, to ask who they were, to ask why they'd come here. He wanted to know if the fishing boats or the Coast Guard had found their families, if they'd been reunited with their loved ones. He had to know what happened. He would not give up on them.

Quickly he locked up the shop and ran up the stairs to the apartment. Teresa jumped as he pushed open the door and he saw she had her mobile in her hand and that her face was still raw from crying.

"I was speaking to Giulia," she told him tearfully, lifting her phone. "And we're all agreed. We want to go to the reception center this evening. We need to see them."

CHAPTER 7

It was only a ten-minute stroll to the reception center; they didn't need the scooter. The lay-bys and verges on the slip road leading up to the place were jam-packed with parked police cars and vans, all crammed in as tightly and as skillfully as the football fans' cars outside the San Paolo stadium when Napoli were playing at home. They had to step into the road to avoid the jutting bumpers.

An elderly couple, hand in hand and both dressed in red fleeces, were walking unsteadily toward them. The Optician winced involuntarily as he saw the man's cheap navy trousers flapping above his anklebone; they were a good three or four centimeters shy of any acceptable length.

"*Buona sera!*"

The couple smiled widely as they approached. They clearly recognized Francesco from somewhere.

They stopped to exchange some pleasantries with him, asking how he was, how his daughter's ice cream parlor was doing. They always bought their ice cream from her, you know, the man assured Francesco, because she was the best in Lampedusa. The Optician caught the woman smiling distinctly at him as if they also knew each other, but he couldn't quite place her. He was sure he had not fitted her with glasses in the last couple of years. He prided himself on having an excellent memory for his customers' faces. He smiled back, uncertain.

The elderly man jabbed his thumb over his shoulder in the direction of the reception center gates and asked wasn't it a terrible business what had happened today with that shipwreck? Police reckoned hundreds had been lost. His voice cracked a little as he talked and his wife patted his arm reassuringly. They'd just come up to deliver some secondhand clothes, he explained, for the survivors. Poor buggers had been left with nothing.

Briefly, Francesco outlined for them what had happened that morning on board *Galata*. How they had seen all those people in the sea and how they had tried to save as many as they could. He provided few details. While Francesco told their tale, the Optician scuffed the toe of his trainer on the ground and watched the patterns he made in the dirt.

They were so shocked, the old couple. The lady whimpered, her hands in front of her mouth while fat tears rolled into the deep crevices of her cheeks. The old chap was crying too, crossing himself and looking up to the heavens, perhaps to thank God for sending *Galata* to the migrants or perhaps, thought the Optician scuffed the toe of his trainer on why the hell God had let the tragedy happen in the first place.

So brave, the old lady said to them. You are all so brave. The Optician didn't look up.

He heard the elderly couple make their excuses and wish everyone a good evening. He lifted his gaze and met the eyes of the old lady, whose head was slightly sloped to one side, studying him. She smiled sympathetically, leaned forward then and squeezed his arm hard.

"God bless, dear," she said and limped off, her hand searching for her husband's.

He remembered who she was, then. She was the woman who'd come to the shop the other day looking for cast-off clothing and shoes. The same woman he had turned away.

He flinched as a large mottled-brown dog slinked passed his right thigh, its thin rat-like tail curling high over its back. It hurried toward the heavy wire gates of the reception center, pawing and rubbing its mangy head on the mesh, trying to attract the guard's attention. The Optician watched a young officer grin as he got up to open the door.

"Cheeky monkey!" he quipped, aiming a pretend kick at the dog's hindquarters. "You just can't get enough of these guys, can you?"

Ignoring his protector, the dog made a beeline for the supper line, trotting toward a group of migrant men who the Optician could see were squatting in the dust, rough army blankets over their shoulders, spooning something from plastic pots. The dog sat down in front of them, licking its black lips expectantly.

As the Optician and his friends approached the gates, the metal doors clanged shut.

"Hey! Wait a minute!" shouted the Optician. "Can you let us in please? We are looking for . . . we are looking for the people who arrived here this morning."

The guard looked at them skeptically.

"Which NGO are you from, then?" he asked, chewing gum as he studied their faces and searched the Optician's chest for an ID badge.

"No, no," said the Optician impatiently, dismissing the idea with his hand. "We're not from any organization. It's just that we . . . we know some of the people who arrived this morning . . . and we need to see them."

Teresa stepped forward.

"We really need to see them urgently," she insisted. "It's very important."

The guard chewed for a while then shrugged.

"Members of the public can't come into the reception center," he said firmly. He drew his head back and shot them a quizzical look.

"Are you journalists? Because if you are, you should know that the mayor has already given a statement on what happened this morning and you won't get any interviews with the migrants, OK?"

"We don't want interviews!" snapped the Optician as the others shifted irritably and muttered protests. "We need to talk to them, OK? Look, we know these people. We . . . we pulled them from the water this morning."

"No can do, mate," said the guard amiably. He took off his cap and swept his hair back from his forehead. "But that was you guys, was it? Well! That was some rescue you pulled off—they reckon hundreds drowned out there today."

He retreated back to his little sentry box, calling over his shoulder that he'd radio the chief to see what he could do.

The Optician and Maria put their fingers through the wire fence and peered at the group of migrants that they could make out in the dusky light eating by the trees. Were they the same people they'd saved? Was it they who had sat weeping on the deck of their boat, gasping the sweet air of life? Teresa and Giulia waved tentatively at the group but the men, intent on eating, seemed to stare through them. No one waved back. As they finished their rations, the asylum seekers casually chucked their plastic pots on the ground and the dog was quick to take his chances, snatching the pots one by one and dragging them a little way off to the tree line to enjoy the scraps alone.

Squinting through the fence like this, it was difficult to make out how the reception center was laid out. On the right-hand side there seemed only to be heavy trees and on the left there were a series of low, nondescript whitewashed buildings that were so uniform and anonymous they might equally be offices or dormitories. In front of the far buildings, scores of police officers in dark-blue uniforms patrolled.

"Chief's busy!" shouted the guard, leaning out of his sentry box. "But the answer is no!" He stepped back inside his sentry box and picked up the phone.

"Hey!" the Optician yelled back. "Don't turn your back on us! Get someone else to come and talk to us—we need to get in!" He rattled the fence. "Hey!"

The guard quietly shut his door.

Steep grassy banks flanked the right-hand side of the path outside the reception center. They were thick with litter. Matteo tried scrambling up but slid back down, his foot skidding on a half-empty pizza box. He cursed and wiped the tomato sauce from his shoe on the coarse foliage before trying again a little farther away from the gates. This time he successfully clambered up to the ridge. He called to the others.

"Come on! Up here we can walk along the side fence and we might be able to see into those buildings."

Small stones cascaded from the face of the dry bank as they climbed up one after the other. The Optician held out his hand to steady Elena who was slipping in her sandals; his heart bounced in his chest as her fingers gripped his.

There was a jumble of discarded clothing on the ridge. A couple of playing cards flapped in the evening breeze, imprisoned in the spikes of tough grass and a small black notebook, swollen and crimped from being waterlogged, fanned its drying pages. Francesco picked it up and leafed through it but its contents had run off the pages. Gabriele drew their attention to a bright red sweatshirt proclaiming the improbable slogan "Welcome to California!"

They gingerly kept going. The Optician felt something rubbery under his tennis shoe and he jumped back with a gasp. He lifted his foot and saw that he'd trodden on the head of a limbless plastic doll whose contorted face, tattooed now with the imprint of his shoe sole, stared up at the sky with a single sea-blue eye. Her left eye had been pushed deep into its socket by the weight of his foot and a battery in her chest cavity bled rusty liquid onto the patchy grass. There was something deeply disturbing about the battered doll. He lagged behind for a couple of seconds. With the top of his foot, he scooped up a dirty pair of shorts and covered the doll's nakedness with them.

The mangy dog started barking furiously the moment they got to the fence, fearing, the Optician imagined, competition for his pasta pots. He raced up at the bank and snarled through the mesh at them, his ragged beard crusty with tomato sauce. The men whom they'd watched eating stopped chatting together and looked up blankly. Maria called down to them in English and a couple of the men raised a hand suspiciously in greeting. They showed no recognition of *Galata*'s crew. It couldn't be them.

They edged farther along the perimeter fence and the dog followed them, growling his displeasure. Gathered under a huge carport structure, hundreds of black men in jogging pants and flip-flops sat slumped dejectedly on concrete benches or leaned against the pillars, yawning. The Optician looked hard at them trying to recognize faces. Maria yelled out again to the men, setting the dog into another frenzied rage. One of the men stirred, glanced up, and then peeled himself from a bench and began to amble his way toward them, slowly scaling the prickly bank in his flip-flops.

"Very sad day," he said in halting Italian. "Many of my countrymen dies and everyone here is crying. You journalists, yes?" They all began to talk over one another in their haste to clarify why they had come. The man clasped his hands together. "God bless you," he said, drawing a small colored wooden crucifix from his pocket. "Here there are many good people who help us. And all we Eritreans say thank you." He kissed the cross. "You were not the first boat to reach them you know," he sighed. "Another boat passed them but it did not stop."

An exclamation of protest rippled through *Galata*'s crew. The Optician clutched the man's T-shirt through the fence. "That's not possible!" he cried out. "That can't be true! Who wouldn't stop when they saw people in trouble?"

They were all pressed close against the fence now.

"No!" protested Gabriele. "No no no!" His skin had a waxy look to it. "Please, no!"

The Eritrean shook his head sadly and was just beginning to speak again when a policeman, alerted by the commotion caused by the dog, blew his whistle sharply. The man hastily scarpered back down the bank to take up his former place on the concrete bench and stared again at the floor. The policeman clapped his hands.

"Get down from there!' he warned. "You're not allowed up there!" It was clear that he wasn't talking to the dog.

A few of his colleagues joined him, curious, and the Optician shouted back down to them, explaining what they were doing and why they were there. His fingers, locked around the mesh of the fence, were white and he pressed his forehead against the plastic green wire.

"I don't care who you are," retorted one of the police officers. "You can't come in here and you can't talk to the illegal immigrants."

The women protested, pleading with the guards to just give them some news about the people they'd rescued. But the guards, shaking their heads very deliberately, were not backing down. Matteo kicked the fence in frustration. The Optician understood the gesture. It felt like they'd lost them all over again.

"Oh please," cried Teresa, coming forward too and holding the fence. "Please just let us see them for five minutes. Just five minutes!" She looked at her husband imploringly.

"It's very important for us," he said, his voice breaking a little. "They're our . . . they're my . . ." He stopped abruptly.

What were they to him? They could not be described as friends; he did not even know their names or where they came from. Yet he felt a bond with them that went way beyond a friendship. And when he had held their hands in his, when he had watched them take their first breaths on *Galata*'s deck, he knew he had got to the very essence of what life meant. They had looked him in the eye and they had chosen to live.

And yet another boat had apparently chosen to leave them in the water? Had sailed past them, shrugging them off, blinking them out of sight? He felt winded by what the Eritrean had told them and he could see his own shock reflected in Francesco's face, in Elena's, in Gabriele's. Did he know them, these people who had not stopped? Did he perhaps eat in their restaurants, shake their hands, did he advise them on choosing the right glasses to match the shape of their faces? He was reminded of a dinner he had once had in Naples with his father when he was a young man, on the cusp of adulthood. It had just been the two of them and his father had spoken to him man to man about how the war had left him disillusioned with human nature. All of us, his father had warned, carry a latent tendency to cruelty and indifference in our hearts; we are all capable of terrible things. But his father's words had seemed irrelevant to his own comfortable postwar generation. Of course the young Optician had seen the images of emaciated bodies festering in putrid concentration camps but they seemed to have nothing to do with the people he knew and mixed with.

He remembered telling his father confidently that such horror was locked safely in the past, that lessons had been learned and he remembered too his father's fond and sad smile. He saw again those thin, naked bodies lying on *Galata's* deck and the shocked, staring eyes.

Teresa gently helped him uncurl his fingers from the wire.

He shrank back at the main gates when he saw a couple of camera crews had arrived and were trying to film the migrants through the mesh. A small group of journalists were arguing heatedly through the gate with a couple of guards. Giulia approached one of the women she knew from the local paper, pressing her for details about what had happened with the fishing boat and Coast Guard. She hurried back to the others.

"They saved about a hundred more!" she exclaimed. "They are all from Eritrea and Somalia. And they found the children!"

One of the male journalists wearing a smart black jacket turned around from the fence as he overheard her conversation. He looked cocky, thought the Optician, a know-it-all.

"They found the children dead," the journalist corrected Giulia. "Most of the women and children were below deck so they all drowned. They were mainly from Eritrea with a few Somalis I think."

He flicked through his writing pad, checking through some scribbled notes.

"And it looks like their boat went down around two this morning so half of those who got out would have just died anyway after that long in the water." The journalist raised his eyebrows. "The migrants have told the police that a boat went past them without stopping. Bound to be an investigation there." He turned over another page. "Police confirm the first boat that started rescuing them didn't spot them till after six apparently."

The Optician caught his sleeve and asked him to clarify the timing of the shipwreck. An ugly image floated to the front of his mind. He saw himself lying on his bunk on board *Galata* this morning, grinning smugly about being on vacation and debating whether he could be bothered to make coffee as he lay on his back listening to the seagulls screeching. Listening to the people screeching. Listening to the drowning desperate people begging for help. People who had been in the water for four hours already.

"Are you locals?" asked the journalist hopefully. "Because apparently it was a group of islanders who were first on the scene and I heard they saved about forty migrants from drowning."

It was Giulia's turn to contradict.

"It was forty-seven," she said firmly. "I know because it was us on that boat."

They were surrounded immediately. Cameras began snapping in their faces; reporters quarreled with one another as they shouldered their way to the front of the scrum. Francesco and Matteo looked bewildered as the man in the black jacket swiftly fixed tiny microphones onto the lapels of their shirts, tucking the wires into their trouser pockets. The questions were fired at them one after another:

"How did you know there was a shipwreck?"

"How did you feel when you first realized what was happening?"

"How did you manage to rescue all those people?"

"How do you feel about the migration problem in Italy?"

Surreptitiously, the Optician edged away from the crowd, pulling Teresa with him. They were both too shy for all this publicity and he was not going to have his sensitive wife subjected to any grilling by these people. He could hear the emotion in his friends' voices as they tried to recount the details of the terrible day into the various microphones. Maria was quavering a little, her staccato account punctuated by deep breaths and sweeps of her hand across her eyes. The questions were incessant.

The Optician turned and looked behind him into the reception center. The mottled-brown dog, sated now with food, had stolen a sock from one of the migrants and was tossing it in the air and chasing it like an oversized puppy, rolling contentedly on his back in the dust. Somewhere in there, in one of those white buildings, were the forty-seven people they had pulled from the water. And that damn stray dog was free to bother and pester them whereas he was being told he had no right to even ask how they were!

On the far side of the path a gentle-looking man of about his own age seemed deep in conversation with a young African asylum-seeker in a Manchester United soccer shirt. The African's head drooped as the older man gently steered him toward the gate and pressed the intercom. When the guard got up to open the gate, the man placed a fatherly hand on the young man's arm and handed him what looked like a little wooden crucifix on a string. Just the same as the one, realized the Optician, that the Eritrean man on the ridge had. The center's gates opened and he watched the man hug the young asylum-seeker to him. The guard waited patiently, showing no sign of irritation and the African sloped off toward the white buildings. Before shutting the gate again, the guard chatted amicably with the man who had given the little cross to the young migrant and shook his hand warmly. The Optician could not hear all their conversation but he caught enough of the Lampedusan dialect to know they were both local. It was clear the man was a regular here.

Watching the young African's bony shoulder blades cut through his football shirt as he walked out of sight, the Optician wondered why he had never visited the reception center until now.

He could hear many more cars pulling up in the lane and the journalists who were still recording flinched as the beeping of locking systems and the slamming of car doors cut rudely into their interviews. They must be double-parked down there, thought the Optician. There's so many of them that they must be blocking one another in, parked back to back. What on earth were they all needed for, these officials and policemen? What did they do? Well, whatever it was, he concluded while looking through the reception center mesh at the migrants still huddled under their blankets, it clearly wasn't enough.

A brusque redhead from a national newspaper tapped him on the arm. She steered him further away from the media scrum and suggested that they have a little talk. All she was really looking for, she explained while tossing back her red curls, was just a really personal account of how it had felt to be on that boat, how it had felt to save everyone.

The Optician looked at her blankly.

"But we didn't save everyone," he responded flatly. The redhead acquiesced that of course they hadn't managed to save everyone, but even so, perhaps he could describe what she imagined must have been an exhilarating feeling when he had rescued people and perhaps what it was like to realize that some people were going to die before he got to them.

"I mean, I'm guessing you had to play God out there, right?" she pressed him impatiently.

All those grasping hands. All those voices begging to be heard. And he had answered the prayers of just forty-seven of them. He searched her face. He could try to answer her questions, he could try to describe his feelings, but she would never really understand his answers. No one would ever really understand, he thought, except for the seven others who were with him on board *Galata*. And they were also all still trying to understand what had happened. He politely declined the interview.

The local paper was clamoring for group photographs and an individual headshot of each of them. The Optician was as reluctant to have his picture taken as he was to answer questions, but he agreed to the photo. He blinked in the photographers' bright lights, his eyes flitting toward the gates of the reception center. Tomorrow, he thought, he would look up Eritrea on the computer.

The next morning he and Teresa were applauded as they walked into their usual cafe for coffee. The waiter flung the newspaper at him. There were photographs of the eight of them on the front page under the giant caption "Lampedusa's Heroes," and a long article which commended their laudable courage.

He studied the pictures and saw eight faces haggard with exhaustion and grief. Francesco, the oldest of them, stared into the lens with an air of great responsibility as a father might do before breaking terrible news to a child. Maria's face was so swollen with sorrow that you wanted to reach out to try to soothe it with your fingertips. Matteo's eyes shone glassy and hostile with hurt.

In her photo, Teresa was half-smiling, looking at the lens with some bewilderment. She seemed to want to ask something; she seemed on the verge of summoning up the courage to beg someone to explain to her what had just happened. He felt his own baldness made his image look more exposed than the others'. His mouth was twisted downward on the right-hand side. Although he was looking directly at the camera through his well-chosen black-rimmed glasses, he looked utterly perplexed.

He folded the paper over angrily. I'm not a damned hero, he thought. I've failed. We've all failed. Us, Italy, Europe—all of us.

CHAPTER 8

It was too windy really; the palm trees were contorted and a white plastic cafe chair that someone had forgotten to tie down was hurtling along the street on its back, but the Optician needed to go running all the same. He had to clear his head.

That morning in the shop, after he had returned from having his coffee, he had sat in front of the computer pretending to do paperwork but was instead looking up every article he could find about Italy's former colony, Eritrea. The whole place, he'd learned, was run like a military garrison; every sixteen-year-old had to join the army and apparently, the poor kids were stuck in the military for life. The girls as well as the boys! He wasn't quite sure why he was being so secretive about what he was doing but each time that he felt Teresa approaching, he flipped the screen back to his anodyne spreadsheets.

He also read about the traffickers in the shop. He read the wretched testimony of migrants who'd fled through the Sahara and he had learned what the traffickers did to those desperate people who dared to dream of Europe. They stole their money and their mobile phones; they beat the men and they raped the women. He remembered the proud-looking woman they had rescued yesterday, the woman in the turquoise T-shirt who had not cried. Did she have anyone to whom she could tell her story, someone who could comfort her? How was it possible these people were so alone?

He picked up the photograph he kept on his desk and smiled at it ruefully. It was a picture of his sons when they were adolescents, roaring with delight on a garish merry-go-round with their mother, radiant with joy at doing something so wonderfully childish, so completely carefree. The Optician closed the shop door behind him and winced at the buffeting wind. He thought of the faces on *Galata*'s deck. Some of those guys he'd pulled from the water had been so young. They were children, really.

He hopscotched his way through the flying ice cream containers and chip bags that were free-wheeling down the street. What family life, what kind of future could those kids have, he wondered, scattered all over their country in military training camps, far away from home and forced to dig in the fields or mend the roads? They were barely paid anything. He hadn't been able to finish the article about what happened to those who were caught running away. Reading about the brutality of Eritrea's prisons made him nauseous.

Mind you, he snorted to himself as he ran past the sheltered terrace of a small cafe where a dozen or so *carabinieri* were kicking back and sipping fruit juice, Lampedusa had started to look like a damned police state itself. Everywhere you went these days on the island, you were greeted with uniforms, truncheons, and guns. It didn't exactly instill an image of welcome.

A police siren began to wail in the distance and two squad cars came speeding over the little hill on the far side of the port, screeching to a dramatic halt as they veered onto the little track leading to the dock at Porto Favaloro. The Optician knew they were waiting for the dive boats to come back from the wreck—he'd seen the Coast Guard's rubber orange dinghies hovering all day over the site of the sinking. Yesterday the fishing boats had apparently come back to port with their decks choked with bodies—how could there still be more out there?

But he had to see. He felt responsible. He knew some officious policeman or other would block him from walking directly onto the quayside at Porto Favaloro, so he jogged down to the narrow strip of dirty sand and through the open flanks of the ship building and the metalyard which faced the quay. He could see the landing strip perfectly from there. Too perfectly.

The bodies were lined up on the concrete quay in plastic sheets the color of green sludge, the same color, he caught himself thinking, as the ground-sheets he had used many years ago when he took his boys camping. Some were in long black body bags, others were zipped up in white ones, like the sacks they used for recycling. A few were wrapped in surgical blue sheets. The bags bulged at the feet and here and there along the line of bodies the plastic was stretched into a pyramid in the middle of the sack as if the hands were clasped together in prayer across the chest. A couple of the sacks were horribly baggy—children.

He wasn't ashamed of crying here. It seemed respectful to cry. He had little respect generally for the shenanigans of the Vatican but this morning on the radio, the Pope had been spot-on when he said today was a day for tears. A disgrace, he had called this tragedy. A disgrace that we should all be ashamed of. He watched the Coast Guard divers swing another heavy dark sack onto the quayside. A big sack, then a medium sack, and then two little sacks.

He kept waiting for the bags to move. He knew it was ridiculous but it seemed impossible that these people didn't exist anymore when their physical presence was still so apparent. He knew how their hands felt. He knew how their thin shoulder blades glinted when the sun hit them. He knew how they quivered with shame to be naked in front of women.

Why weren't they all laid in the same direction? The first in the line had been placed with his head facing the sea, the next faced the concrete steps. Green, blue, black, and white. It was a gruesome tessellation of death.

He smelled cigarette smoke and realized that he was no longer alone on the scrub of beach. Lost in his thoughts, he had not heard the police diver's boots on the coarse sand. He greeted him and the diver nodded politely. His focus was also on the line of bodies laid out on the dock.

"Nearly two hundred now," he said and took a drag on his cigarette. "I'm used to seeing horrors . . . but this? This is . . ." His face trembled as he fought back tears.

'"I pulled out two little kids of maybe two and three years old from the cabin," he told the Optician. "It was pitiful; they were wearing new shoes. Can you imagine? Their mom had bought them new shoes."

He nipped out his cigarette with his finger and thumb and immediately began to search his pockets for another one. The two men sat on the stumps of the breakwater with their chins supported in their hands and the Optician confessed that he'd been out on the water yesterday, had been the first on the scene. He jerked his thumb toward the bodies.

'"Weren't fast enough, were we?" the Optician asked bitterly. He had meant it as a rhetorical question but the diver answered it anyway, explaining to the Optician that those below deck would not have stood a chance. He seemed to anticipate the Optician's next question.

"Don't know how long they'd have had," he added. "Not long . . . but enough time I think to understand what was coming. You see . . ." He hesitated for a long moment and let his foot tap against the wooden breakwater. "You see, they were all holding hands."

There had been a young woman, the diver said, dressed in a very white shirt and black trousers who was jammed against the cabin stairwell, blocking the door. When his buddy had yanked her arm to free her body, she had concertinaed and then sprung back, bringing with her a string of other bodies all joined at the hands. It was like they'd become one giant singular entity, the diver said. Like a Christmas paper chain. There'd been a heavily-pregnant woman, too. And mothers whose arms still circled their little ones protectively, hugging them safe.

Who were they all? Did their families even know they'd left their homelands? Even though his own boys were in their twenties now, Teresa always expected them to tell her if they were traveling anywhere and to clock in with her again to report that they'd arrived. And yet here were all these people, hundreds of them, anonymous in colored sacks, known only as the woman in the white shirt and the toddler in the patent leather shoes.

"I'd better get back," said the diver, getting up. "The least we can do is bring them to shore." He looked closely at the cigarette butt in his fingers for a moment and then held it up in the air, showing it to the Optician. He smiled ironically.

"I gave this up five years ago," he said.

Back on the road, the Optician picked up the pace. He ran harder and faster than usual, forcing his body to cut through the wind. He could feel the shock of each footfall ricocheting through his vertebrae as his sneakers pounded down on the tarmac. Wheezy little clouds of dust and fine sand blowing in from the coastal road made him cough and spit and his eyes smarted with the grit.

The pity of those body bags! In life they had been robbed of a future and in death they'd been robbed of an identity.

He was inside the graveyard before he had made a conscious decision to visit it. He'd been thinking about the body bags when suddenly there he was among the dense labyrinth of headstones, family vaults, and mausoleums—all blanched by the strong sun.

They were beautifully kept up, these graves; the gold and black lettering chiseled deep into the stone, small steel pots packed with dried flowers and weighted with bricks against the wind's caprices standing guard at the foot of the tombs. Oval-shaped photographs that were glued to the marble prompted visitors to remember who the occupants had been. Here was eighty-two-year-old Rosa, smiling over a birthday cake; she'd been joined the following year by her husband, Antonio, a retired doctor, wearing a red sweater with a butterscotch-colored cat in his arms. Andrea in the next plot had had a distinguished military career—in the 1940s wedding photograph with his wife, Anna, his chest was already festooned with medals. Their son joined them twenty years later. The Optician brushed away the husk of a dried flower to read the inscription. He'd been a marine biologist, apparently.

He walked the graveyard quietly, stopping every now and then when he spotted a name that registered with him or a headstone that intrigued him. He stooped to set upright a stainless steel pot of flowers that the wind had skittled. In the distance he could hear a tuneless whistling and the slow slapping sound of someone walking in flip-flops.

Halfway down the cemetery, he saw on his right a small unkempt patch of wasteland and he approached it curiously. The sandy earth was cracked dry and the fissures in the ground were choked with yellow dandelions and spiky sea grasses and gorses. A couple of flimsy wooden crosses planted in a powdery block of cement were trembling as they fought against the wind to stay rooted; many others had lost their battle and were lying facedown in the thorn bushes. He turned one over with his foot and saw the number eight had been inked on the join in faded black paint.

The slapping sound of the feet stopped beside him. An unshaven older man in a gray polo shirt flecked with white paint appeared and put down a shovel and a bucket of plaster.

"Poor buggers," he said to the Optician, chewing at his bottom lip with his one remaining tooth. "I've worked in this graveyard for thirty years but I always nod to them when I pass."

The Optician looked at him blankly.

"The migrants," the man explained matter-of-factly. "The unknown migrants who drown off Lampedusa. I've buried them all. I'm the grave-digger here."

The gravedigger began to pick at pieces of plaster that had lodged under his fingernails. The Optician looked down at the shovel and felt himself recoil. A vision of the sludge-green body bags lined up on the quayside floated back into the Optician's mind. Is this where they would end up? Dumped in a patch of weeds with a piece of unvarnished wood flung on top of them as an afterthought?

The gravedigger told him there were at least sixty migrant graves in the cemetery, squeezed in, he said, wherever they could find a space. Sometimes you could pop them on top of a long-gone family's vault; you couldn't do it with the tombs of those who still had visitors at the family graves of course—they wouldn't appreciate a cuckoo in the nest. The poor souls who had drowned yesterday wouldn't be buried here though; there were too many of them; more than two hundred, he'd heard the mayor say on the radio just now—she'd appealed for coffins. They'd be shipped off to Sicily unless their relatives claimed them. Fat chance of that happening, he said, scratching the white stubble on his chin.

He led the Optician to a plot around the corner, wheezing as he walked, his calloused heels in his flip-flops split as deeply as the dry earth.

"Buried him a few weeks back," he said gruffly, rubbing his rough hand over a large gray patch of concrete at the top of a stack. "Young boy. About seventeen, they reckon. Probably Eritrean. Drowned in a dinghy."

The Optician edged forward. The Eritrean boy was sharing his vault with a mustachioed man who peered out sternly from his photograph in a gasoline-colored suit and navy tie. A pastel painting of the Madonna looked down on the mustachioed man protectively. Over his right shoulder two fluttering *putti* had been carved onto the stonework, watching him with adoration. The attentive, careful details rendered the blankness of the crude cement patch above him truly pathetic. It looked, thought the Optician, like the boy had been deliberately effaced, censored from existence.

The gravedigger seemed to know what he was thinking.

"I might not know his name," he growled fiercely. "But I remember him. Believe me, I remember them all."

The wind had begun to amuse itself by picking up plastic watering cans and bouquets of dead flowers, racing them along the narrow alleyways between the gravestones and then flinging them to the ground, where they spun exhausted on the grit walkways. A large piece of jagged white plastic was cartwheeling toward them and the gravedigger stopped it with his foot. He picked it up and cursed.

"It was loose and now the wind's torn it off the grave," he said, handing it to the Optician and then stamping off furiously. The Optician looked at the flimsy plastic panel and read what he could of the incomplete inscription.

"Here lies the body of an unknown . . .

Drowned off the coast of Lampe . . .

Believed to be from the Horn of A . . .

He was aged around twenty."

He found the gravedigger in front of a marble mausoleum where he was propping up the remaining half of the panel with a pot of borrowed flowers and a small rock of old concrete. The wind had spitefully torn the cheap plastic board in two.

"Why are they left to rot like this?" asked the Optician incredulously. "Why does no one care for them?"

The gravedigger wheeled around quickly and snarled at the Optician, his eyes wide with anger.

"Why are they left to *die* like this?" he snapped. "You answer me *that* question!"

He snatched the shard of plastic from the Optician and waved it at him.

"Why does Europe do the minimum possible to stop this? You tell me that!" He rolled his *r*'s dramatically. "God knows it makes me *furious!*"

The Optician could not answer him. He held the plastic panel together while the gravedigger blocked the two halves with the pot and a couple of rocks. The Optician stared at the fractured plaque. Unknown and uncared for. These people seemed to be no one's problem.

The gravedigger pressed his palm flat against the stone.

"Each time you bury one you hope it's the last," he said. "You always hope it will be the last." He picked up his bucket of plaster, nodded politely to the Optician, and trudged off, sighing.

It felt suddenly cold in the graveyard and the Optician decided to cut his run short and head home. He was still physically spent from yesterday and the nervous energy that had been fueling him until now was beginning to cool in his veins, leaving him feeling heavy-limbed and slightly queasy. As he jogged slowly back to port, he thought of the grave-digger's words.

Why wasn't more being done to stop these tragedies? It had been pure chance that *Galata* had been in the right place at the right time. Yet everyone knew these refugee boats kept traveling to Lampedusa and Sicily so why weren't there professional search-and-rescue teams on permanent duty?

His head, normally calm and empty on this homeward stretch, was teeming with questions.

Maria and Francesco were in the shop with Teresa when he got back and they fell on him when he entered.

"We've been invited to a service tomorrow!" beamed Teresa. "The mayor's office called to invite us all—we'll be able to see them again—they'll all be there." She took his hand and squeezed it. "We can see them again!"

Francesco filled in the details. It was to be a service of remembrance and reflection in a hangar at the airport where the coffins were being stored. All the survivors would be there, all the rescue workers were to go and the mayor and some politicians. It was to be a brief service before the bodies were transferred to Sicily and there would be a minute's silence to honor the dead.

Maria was emotional. "And can you believe it," she said, "our government in Rome has announced that each of the dead is to be given a state funeral!" She smiled at Teresa. "We've been talking about it just now—it's a sign that everything is going to change."

The Optician smiled back at them thinly. He thought of the cheap plastic panel, sheared off by the wind on the grave of the drowned young migrant and of all the nameless, trampled wooden crosses that the bindweed seemed determined to suffocate. State funerals were truly a grand gesture. A grand gesture of a guilty conscience. He tried to imagine the coffins draped in the red, white, and green of the Italian flag, a military band playing while soldiers carried the caskets to a well-chosen spot of a shady graveyard to lay them to rest together in their own mausoleum. Call him cynical, but he just couldn't imagine it. He just couldn't. He forced himself to keep smiling.

CHAPTER 9

The Optician had always associated the airport
with excitement—didn't everybody? For him and for
Teresa the airport meant catching a plane. It meant
going back to Naples to see the boys, it meant family
dinners, it meant laughter and fun. Vacations.

There wasn't a breath of laughter left now.
Galata's crew walked to the airport hangar
together in silence, their arms linked. They were
all desperate to see the people they had saved but
they were also terrified of seeing the coffins. Teresa
was worried that she would not recognize those
they had helped. How rude and dismissive it would
seem, she said to her husband, if she could not
pick out their faces from all the other migrants! He
was cursing the fact that he did not speak English
or whatever language they spoke. He wanted to
explain to them that they had tried so hard to get

to see them before now, that they had been worrying about them, that they had repeatedly called the hospital for news about those who had needed treatment. But how did you convey the message "we have never stopped thinking of you" in sign language? How did you explain that it was the complex bureaucracy of migration rules that had prevented them from coming to visit them in the reception center? He was so anxious to make them understand how hard they had tried, that they had not forgotten them for one second.

But at the event there was no awkwardness. The migrants were waiting for them, watching for them outside the entrance to the hangar. As they approached, they ran to them eagerly like primary school children meeting their parents at the end of the school day, clamoring to greet them with their arms outstretched. The women folded the migrants against their chests and rocked them. Big men, some nearly two meters tall, cuddled as little boys do, heads bent to Teresa's shoulder, nestled on Maria's neck, weeping.

He had never been good at reaching out to people. He was not one of those types who touched people while talking to them, laying a hand on a knee or a shoulder. Teresa always said he was so uncomfortable at physical contact with strangers that he could appear cold. Yet when the first young man took his hand and squeezed it tight in thanks, it wasn't enough; it felt insipid. So the Optician forcibly pulled the boy toward him and locked him in a fierce embrace. He didn't want to let the boy go. He didn't want to let any of them go.

It didn't matter that they didn't share a language. They seemed to understand how worried *Galata*'s crew had been as to how they were faring. Some gave them the thumbs-up sign to reassure them that they were OK, then inclined their heads on their open palms to indicate they were just very tired. One of the teenagers took the Optician's hand and held it over his breast so that the Optician could feel the thumping of his heart. He smiled at the Optician and pointed his finger at him. The Optician understood the message. You gave me life, he was saying. You gave me my life.

He told them his name and they rolled the strange syllables around their mouths shyly, tasting the sound. They told him their names, but there were so many of them that he caught only the melody and not the particulars. He tried to count their numbers as they swirled around him and Teresa. Forty-two, forty-three . . .

He watched them line up respectfully to embrace Francesco. They recognized that Francesco was the boss, as the oldest, and they understood that it had been his boat that had saved them. They looked at him with awe as if he were a god or a holy prophet. Father, they said as they kissed his hand. Our Father.

They were wearing incongruous clothes for this solemn occasion. The reception center had obviously kitted them out with whatever was around and they looked almost as raggedy as they had on *Galata*. Trousers hung loosely from their narrow hips, held up by stringy bits of blue nylon cord and many were wearing T-shirts proclaiming allegiance to Italian football teams which the Optician doubted they had ever heard of. Most were in tennis shoes but those who'd clearly been at the back of the line had to make do with the leftover mismatched flip-flops. One forlorn man was wearing a pair of ladies' furry bedroom slippers with the pompom missing from the right foot. In another life, thought the Optician, it might have been funny. Right now it was so pathetic that he wanted to take off his own shoes and offer the man his dignity.

Thirteen thousand asylum seekers had arrived in Italy so far this year, Gabriele had told them when he'd come to fetch them in the car to take them to the air hangar. Until now this had just been a random, meaningless figure. An empty statistic. Yet here they were before them, flesh and blood, bone and gristle and the salt of their tears mingling. Boys with names that sounded like music, men whose hearts thumped with life and promise. Names—not numbers! Names!

There were a handful of women survivors by the door but he recognized the girl they'd saved immediately because of her long dreadlocks. They splayed out from under a small black scarf she had placed over her head. A long black shirt had replaced her turquoise T-shirt but she still wore her old look of pride. He wanted to hold her but it was clear she was terrified of anyone coming close.

When Elena tried to hug her she voiced her gratitude politely and sincerely, in both English and Italian, but she stood stiffly in Elena's arms and did not allow herself to be scooped into an embrace like the men did. What force she must have to keep from tears! He, Matteo, Francesco, and Gabriele could do nothing to temper their emotions.

It was Maria who spotted the girl's hands. She saw the girl's discomfort at being held too close, so when it was her turn to speak to her, she simply took the girl's hands in hers. The girl winced in pain. When Maria lifted the girl's hands to examine them, Maria cried out herself. The pads of her fingers were singed red and black. Bulbous yellow blisters grew on top of the deep burns.

"Who hurt you darling, who hurt you?" asked Maria, her voice panicky, her hand touching the woman's face.

The girl shrugged and pulled a lighter and the remnants of a supermarket carrier bag from her jeans pocket.

"No fingerprints, please," she explained with an embarrassed smile. "Please, no fingerprints."

He was heartsick at what she had done. He had read in the paper that migrants sometimes tried to destroy their fingerprints. It was to get around some EU rule that demanded refugees must claim asylum in the first safe country they arrived in. But he had never thought through what that actually meant. He winced, looking at the swollen blisters. He asked Teresa if she had a tube of arnica gel in her bag, forgetting for a second that the boys had long grown up and Teresa no longer had any need to carry medicines for them anymore.

He held the girl gently by the wrists and studied her burned hands, shaking his head. He recalled suddenly the image of that horrible doll he had trodden on in the grass outside the reception center, with its trampled, battered face and bleeding battery cavity. The brutality of this whole damned system! Hadn't these people suffered enough, weren't they damaged enough without having to resort to this? He was too distressed to say anything to the young woman. He wanted to ask her where she was planning to go and whether she had family there waiting for her, but he couldn't trust his voice to stay strong. He looked her in the eye for a long moment, hoping she would know that he wished her well, that he was telling her he would never forget her. She melted away from him.

Inside the hangar, the coffins were spaced with military precision, each exactly one meter from its neighbor. A single red rose had been laid on the lid of every burnished-mahogany casket. There were over a hundred of them. And fronting the sickening parade were four tiny white coffins. These were decorated with a small, smiling teddy bear in a blue and white striped T-shirt with a love heart in the center of his chest. In two of these caskets lay the toddlers that the diver had said were wearing brand new patent leather shoes. The Optician pulled at a loose thread on the sleeve cuff of his jacket and twisted the thread around his finger tightly, trying to stem the volcano of emotions that were now brewing inside him. He did not think he would have the courage to stay for the service.

Matteo stared at the far wall of the hangar, plucking nervously at his beard. The Optician noticed that he would not look at the caskets. Just before the service started, Matteo leaned over and whispered:

"Last week, before we rescued these people, did you know that thirteen people drowned off the coast of Sicily? I barely registered the news. I barely gave them a thought."

So he was not alone, then, in feeling this guilt.

For the remembrance service, they were asked to stand with the members of the emergency services, with the Coast Guard and the fishermen who had joined the rescue efforts. He was glad for that now, looking at the migrants as they faced the coffins. Some were bent over double with grief, squatting on the floor, their heads between their knees, while three of the surviving women were keening the same terrible death wail that they had heard from the boat. This ceremony was theirs: it was for those who had died and for those who had survived and it would have felt intrusive to be standing in the middle of such profound, personal grief. He could hear Teresa gasping as she tried to temper her own distress and he dared not look at her as he took her hand. He was thankful that the television cameras had not been allowed inside to film this intimate moment.

He tried to concentrate on the service, breathing in the musky scent of incense and the wisps of smoke from the candles. An imam and a Catholic priest were taking turns singing verses and chanting prayers, their voices sounding thin and reedy as they bounced off the immense walls of the huge aircraft hangar. And although he didn't believe in any of this religious stuff, he felt something stir inside him at the beauty of the haunting sounds and the solemnity of it all. It felt holy and pure and unique. He would stay. He would make himself stay. He owed the migrants that.

There must have been two or three hundred people circled around the coffins—yet how tiny and insignificant they seemed in all this space! He imagined the men in suits must be politicians from Rome and Sicily. They stood like soldiers with their backs exaggeratedly straight, mumbling responses to the prayers, occasionally crossing themselves. Their own mayor had her face buried in a handkerchief and the Optician could see that her whole body was shaking.

It sounded like poetry when the priest read out the long list of the dead. Exotic names washed over his head like waves. He couldn't tell where one name ended and a new one began. Efrem, Asmeret, Gaim, Biniam, Niyat, Senait. Somewhere in the world, mothers would be polishing framed photographs of these lost sons and daughters, waiting anxiously for a phone call to reassure them that they had arrived safely.

He watched the woman he'd rescued blowing on her burned fingers. What was her name? Was her brother in one of these caskets? He imagined the two of them plotting, mustering the courage to take this adventure together, taking comfort in the knowledge that whatever happened on the journey, at least they would be together to pursue their dreams in this new promised land.

He forced himself to look at the forlorn survivors. They would have visualized only positive things for their new life in the place they thought was Paradise. Everything would be fresh and exciting in Europe and they expected only laughter and jobs, safe homes and freedom. Now, he could see that fable unwinding and peeling away from them like the colored paint on the cracked hulls of the wrecks that he had seen rotting by the port. He squeezed his eyes shut to try to stop the tears. He felt useless. Yes, he had saved them—but for what kind of future? All their delightful fantasies had curdled and spoiled and they did not know how to create a new dream to believe in. No one had told them that in Europe, in Paradise, people also suffered and were wretched.

He became conscious that one of the young men he had rescued was watching him. He hastily wiped the sleeve of his jacket over his eyes. The teenager continued to look at him, his mouth slightly open. It was the same desperately expectant look that they had all given him when they were in the water. Save me. Help me. Please.

The Optician clasped his hands together. Was he praying? Is this what prayer was? He glanced at Francesco whose head was bent low. He wasn't sure if Francesco was a believer. They'd never talked about things like that. Gabriele was biting his knuckles. He looked feverish. Giulia was whispering words, her fingers pulling hard at her dangling turtle earrings. He took Teresa's candle from her—she was sobbing so much that the hot wax was dropping onto her hand and burning her. She kept asking him the same question: were the police sure who the children's mothers were so that they could be buried together? She was so distressed to see the little coffins apart like that—the mothers wouldn't want to be separated from their children, she kept insisting. They ought to be placed side by side.

He had not told Teresa what the police diver had said about finding the drowned woman hugging her little ones to her body, about the children's new shoes. He did his best to reassure her, but what did he know? He suspected that the unnamed would be buried beside strangers in a country they had dreamed of but had never gotten the chance to know.

All day, the divers had been under the water harvesting corpses, sorting through the jumble of tangled limbs on the dark seabed and tying the bodies together with rigging rope before dragging them back up into the light. He had gone to the port to buy prawns from the fishmongers, but afterward he had turned right instead of left, drawn back in spite of himself to the little strip of coarse sand that faced the Coast Guard's landing strip. It wasn't prurience; he still clung to the ludicrous hope that someone would have been found alive and that he could go home to Teresa to tell her some good news. He wanted desperately to give Teresa some good news. But as he crossed through the ship building yard and onto the patch of rough beach, he saw the hunched figure of the police diver sitting on the breakwater, his arms crossed protectively over his head as if to ward off blows, his back sporadically hiccupping. Respectfully, he had backed away.

The service came to an end, and thank God because he needed air.

Perhaps tomorrow, perhaps even right now, another rickety, unseaworthy boat was being stuffed with frightened migrants on the Libyan coast and was making its uncertain way to Lampedusa. He swallowed. And how many of them would make it?

As they filed out, he felt a sudden desperate urge to get away from all this death, from these coffins and this heart-wrenching pervasive sadness that he could do nothing about. He wanted to run home to rewind the tape of the past few days, to press pause at the point where they had all boarded *Galata* and to erase that part and put another scene in its place. *Aperitivi* at that awful loud bar Matteo liked instead, or a humble picnic down at Rabbit Beach, or a pistachio ice cream at Francesco's daughter's place. Anything, anything but this.

Teresa pulled on his arm. He knew she wanted to say goodbye to the four little white coffins.

He walked with her. The teddies smiled cheerfully at them, oblivious.

They were not given long to say goodbye to the refugees after the service. The police wanted them back in the reception center quickly. Many of the migrants were reluctant to leave their dead. Two of the women had to be pulled off the coffin lid. They were still wailing their sorrow as they were escorted to the police van.

Parting from them was indescribable. The roar of emotion inside him frightened the Optician. He did not feel in control. As they hugged goodbye he was aware of hearing strange animalistic noises and even afterward, when he was back home and away from it all, he was not sure if the cries had come from Francesco, from one of the others, or from himself. He just wanted to save them. He wanted to save them from whatever came next.

The survivors spoke urgently in their own language and in snatches of English, clutching at them, clinging to them. He understood nothing except the words "thank you." But he could feel what they wanted to say.

As the police van backed out of the car park, its headlights caught them full in the face. For a brief second, he saw the crumpled, tearstained faces of Gabriele and Francesco and he saw wet tracks coursing down Matteo's cheeks. It was the first time he had ever seen his friends cry.

They sat up late that night, he and Teresa. You couldn't sleep after something like that. The last three days had been the most emotionally intense experience of his entire life, of all of their lives. His wife looked battered by the shock and he supposed he did too. One of his customers that morning asked him if he were ill. He hadn't exactly led a charmed life, he'd suffered his own losses, had his own moments of pain, but he had had no idea that such profound depths of sorrow existed. He could never imagine feeling such an acute sadness again.

Teresa wanted to see the news and he switched on the television reluctantly, not wanting her to be exposed again to the awful images of the coffins. He sat up in his chair, jolted. The police diver to whom he'd been talking the day before was being interviewed on the quayside with the arms of his dive buddies draped protectively round his shoulders.

That evening, the diver was saying falteringly, wedged right into the prow of the ship, he found a very young woman clutching a bundle of rags. He had swum to her and when he pulled at the bundle, the cloth had fallen away to reveal a tiny baby boy.

His mask had fogged up with tears and he had nearly choked. Because he realized the baby was still attached to his mother by the umbilical cord.

How naïve he'd been, thought the Optician. How naïve. Because there would always be greater sorrow, deeper and more unfathomable than any of us could ever imagine.

CHAPTER 10

The Optician worried about Teresa's nightmares. More than two weeks had passed since they had rescued those people at sea and her nightmares seemed to be getting worse with time, not better. They had all had them. They'd been quite open with each other about the effects of the trauma on their mental states.

Gabriele admitted he was suffering from insomnia. His skin was permanently the color of tracing paper now and his denim-blue eyes looked bleached and faded. Elena, Matteo, and Francesco were struggling with their anger. Elena had fought with her boss on the telephone, Matteo had blown up at his girlfriend and then broken up with her. Giulia and Maria felt down and depressed. Maria seemed to shrink into herself, hunkering down into the folds of her rigging-rope scarf while Giulia's wayward hair had become unkempt and wild. But Teresa's suffering was truly terrible. She'd wake up choking, not able to breathe, sobbing and clutching at imaginary figures.

They'd even had to go the hospital in the middle of the night last week. Panic attacks, the doctor said. She needed to talk it out with someone, but he found it so difficult to relive those awful hours on the water. Once, she had been so distracted that she had appeared in the shop in her dressing gown. She had looked at him curiously when he ushered her back upstairs as if he was someone she knew yet couldn't quite place. When he'd scolded her for coming downstairs in her nightwear, when he'd tried to explain that it would have been truly embarrassing for them both if a client had been in the shop when she'd appeared like that, she had merely searched his face with her emerald-green eyes as if she were trying to decipher a deeper message.

He didn't tell her, but the shipwreck played in his own head when he slept like a film on a loop. The pictures were in glorious Technicolor but the most terrifying thing was that the images were completely silent. He could see migrants begging for help and he could see Francesco with his mouth stretched wide, yelling something at him. But he couldn't hear what anyone was saying—he couldn't even hear the sea—he just stood there, frozen, not knowing what to do while the heads sank under the waves.

If he was honest, it didn't just happen at night while he slept.

The problem was that the sadness just would not go away. The coffins had been removed to Sicily and almost all of the survivors had been transferred to the mainland but the sadness lingered like the wispy October fog which crept in from the sea each morning, its damp fingers chilling and pervasive.

A new source of sorrow had even arrived to fill the vacuum left by the coffins. Relatives of the dead and missing already in Europe had come to Lampedusa to identify bodies and to try to establish if their family members had indeed been on that fateful boat. They sat hunched in the cafes and bars of the island; representatives of a lucky diaspora who had already made the trip and who had benevolently funded the ill-fated journeys of the dead.

At lunch time, these relatives kept watch outside the *carabinieri* station near the Optician's shop, throwing themselves at anyone in uniform who went in or out, pressing them for information and pushing photographs of their missing into policemens' hands. He'd seen some of the relatives standing at the gates by Porto Favaloro, stalking the quayside, ready to pounce on the police divers and the search-and-rescue crews when they docked. They followed the police and the divers to the cafes and the bars too. Once, while he and Teresa were having their morning coffee, he had seen a police diver hesitate while looking at a photograph pushed urgently in front of his face as he sat eating breakfast with a colleague. The diver wiped the greasy *arancini* from his face with a tissue, took the picture, and studied it closely, whispering conspiratorially with his colleague. They left the food uneaten and gently led the woman with the photograph out of the bar and into their pick-up truck outside, presumably to take her to the morgue. But that only happened once; usually the police and the divers just scratched their chins before shaking their heads apologetically and walking away.

The diaspora met in Francesco's ice cream parlor too, frantic. From his bar stool at the counter, the Optician watched them shouting into mobile phones in their own languages, in English, in Arabic, in Italian, in German. Their tables were strewn with photographs and tatty pieces of paper. They hung up calls dejectedly and struck through phone numbers on their notepads or paper napkins, jotting down new ones and scribbling notes.

A young African man in trendy ripped jeans noticed the concern of Francesco and the Optician and came over to introduce himself. He was a languages student at Munich university, he said, and although he had left Eritrea with his parents when only a baby, he felt it was his duty to come to Lampedusa to help the relatives search and to translate for them. They were calling the traffickers, he explained, nodding to the relatives, to see if their niece, their nephew, or their missing cousin had been a passenger on that boat. He translated conversations for them in a low whisper.

"He was probably wearing a denim jacket," shouted one man hopelessly, pushing his reading glasses onto the top of his head and rubbing his eyes. "And he has a crescent-shaped scar on his left cheek." He held the photograph up to the light. "No, wait! He has the scar on his right cheek. Do you remember him boarding at Misrata? He's eighteen but maybe he looks a bit older?"

Some were well dressed and clearly educated. His former tailor's eye spotted the well-cut lines of a beige Armani jacket on an East African woman of near enough his own age who kept pausing her conversations with the traffickers to take business calls in Italian on another mobile phone.

"Her mom says she always wore a ring in the shape of a coiled snake. Does that jog your memory at all? We haven't heard from her in two weeks now and we believe she was heading to Misrata. Please?"

The Optician almost wished the student would stop translating for them.

To hear these desperate people asking favors from unfeeling criminals turned his stomach. He sipped his espresso and the taste was bitter.

The captain of the boat had been arrested. Some of the migrants they saved had recognized him at the reception center and reported him to the police. He was a Tunisian, apparently, who had already been deported once from Italy and was part of a large trafficking ring. The migrants said they'd been beaten for complaining about the claustro-phobic conditions on board the boat. When some of the women had not been able to come up with all the fare that was being demanded from them, they'd been raped. While they were reading the story together in the paper, Francesco lifted his eyebrows to the Optician, and said simply, "The girl. The girl we rescued."

More than three hundred and fifty corpses had now been recovered and the police diving teams were still looking. There was another shipwreck this week between Malta and Lampedusa: Syrians this time, and Palestinians. Thirty-four of them had drowned before the Coast Guard could get to them. The Optician twisted the elastic top of his sock and let it snap back. This stretch of the Mediterranean between Lampedusa and Libya was turning into a graveyard.

Yesterday morning, he'd been at the fish-mongers when the night boats had come in with their haul. While he was waiting for his fish to be wrapped, he chatted politely to the fishermen as they unloaded, asking them whether they had a good catch. One of the fishermen took off his oilskin and told him he couldn't take the stress anymore, profit or no profit. He was going to retire early and move to Palermo, he explained, to be with his son's family. It wasn't just the fear that he'd find himself out at sea in the middle of a migrant shipwreck, he said, it was the fear of what he might find in his nets when he pulled them up.

The man with the reading glasses sitting near the counter hung up his phone and slumped forward in his chair, his elbows on the table, his head in his hands. They didn't need the Eritrean student to tell them it was bad news. The Optician looked away quickly. Maybe if they had been faster out there on the sea, maybe if he'd noticed the screaming more quickly, this poor man would never have come to Lampedusa to undertake such a hideous task. His relative would have been safe on *Galata*'s deck, with the women fussing over him, finding him clothes and water. He kicked the leg of his bar stool. Why had the Coast Guard made them stop? Why had they been forced to turn their backs? He was sure they could have saved more. He rubbed the pulsating vein above his right ear. One boat had passed those desperate people and had not stopped at all. How did that boat's crew sleep at night?

The woman in the Armani jacket raised her voice and was thumping the table in frustration as she talked on the phone.

"Sounds like the trafficker wants more money for the information," sighed the student. "He seems to be telling her he *might* have information but she'll need to help him out a bit."

It was all so ugly. Everywhere was ugly. The state funeral promised for the dead had been downgraded to a "solemn ceremony" in Agrigento. The survivors had not even been invited. There was no special memorial mausoleum for the drowned: they were scattered in cemeteries across Sicily. Who knew where those who had been buried without names were now? They had been found in the depths of the sea and brought back into the light, but on land they had been lost again.

And the survivors? The Optician rubbed his hands up and down the thighs of his pants. He felt sick when he thought about the survivors and their future. A couple of them had taken down Francesco's email address but there'd been no news so far. Francesco fiddled with the computer constantly; if challenged he said he was checking stuff for his carpentry work, but the Optician knew what his friend was looking for. Poor Francesco. Every time they met, they looked at him expectantly and he sighed and shook his head.

There were rumors that the survivors could be fined thousands of euros for entering Italy illegally. Fined! Which planet did these lawmakers come from? The prime minister had come to Lampedusa the other day and visited the reception center. He must have seen the desperate state these migrants were in. The center was running at three or four times its capacity; some refugees had to sleep outdoors. He thought of the pitiful man

they'd rescued who had been wearing the ladies'
bedroom slippers at the memorial service. Where
did the politicians imagine he had hidden his
supposed wealth to pay such a fine? These people
had nothing. They did not even have their dream
to cling to anymore.

Francesco passed him another espresso and
play-punched his cheek. The Optician attempted
a smile. He wasn't stupid; he knew that Europe
couldn't possibly welcome every single person who
fancied a better life for himself, but there had to be
some alternative to this mess. He knew from his
Internet research that most Eritreans who arrived
in Europe were automatically granted asylum:
abject poverty, years of war, and a military dic-
tatorship were hard for any EU country to argue
against. So why make them go through this treacherous journey? It was like a sinister selection test:
manage this deadly assault course successfully
and bingo . . . you've earned yourself a place in
Paradise. Matteo teased him that he sounded like
a politician when he talked like that; he should run
for mayor, he joked drily when they met for a beer
last week. But the Optician hated politics. Politics
was all about self-interest. This wasn't about
politics anyway; it was about humanitarianism.

It was about anticipating the desperate hands in the water and acting before they got there.

The woman in the nice jacket collected her things together from the table and stuffed them into her canvas travel bag. She approached the bar and settled her bill with Francesco. Gently, he wished her luck with her search.

"I have to fly back to Rome in a couple of hours," she said in perfect Italian, shaking her head. She unzipped the top of her bag and pulled out a photograph.

"I'm looking for her," she said, handing the photo to Francesco. He tilted it so the Optician could see the picture too.

It was a headshot of a pretty girl in her late teens or very early twenties who had close-cropped hair and a wide, red-lipsticked smile. She was wearing a pale-blue, low-cut satin blouse and a lot of makeup. A silver crucifix dangled in her cleavage. The woman looked at the picture fondly.

"She's my second cousin. This picture was taken a couple of years ago when she was at home in Asmara," she explained. "There was a family party because she had a week's leave from the military."

Francesco muttered some appropriately kind words. The woman shrugged. "I haven't seen her since she was five," she explained. "I send her family money a few times a year and her mom sends me photographs by way of return." She nodded her approval when Francesco asked if he could pass the photograph to the Optician. "I sent her the funds to flee Eritrea and her uncle in Sweden wired what she needed for the boat crossing from Libya. That's where she was heading, you see, to Sweden. We're almost certain she was in the boat that sank."

She shuddered. The police had asked her to study some photographs of the drowned women but their faces were so puffy and swollen with water that she had not liked to linger on the images. In any case, she had not recognized her cousin.

The Optician scrutinized the laughing girl in the picture again. Done up to the nines like that, it was easy to imagine her about to head off for an evening out in Naples or Palermo, perhaps on a date with a boyfriend. She did not look like a pitiful refugee, she looked ordinary; the type of good-looking girl you passed on the street all the time. She had simply been born in the wrong place, poor kid.

He handed the woman back the photograph and asked her awkwardly, his eyes lowered, what her cousin's name was.

"Saba," said the woman. "Her name is Saba."

A pretty name, Saba, the Optician said quietly. He would have liked to be able to turn to the woman, to touch her arm and to say to her, excuse me but yes, I remember this girl! I saved her! I pulled your cousin onto my boat! Instead, he swiveled away from her on his bar stool and twisted the elastic of his sock more tightly around his finger as Francesco began to unpack the glasses from the dishwasher.

No. He had not saved Saba. And he had not saved the man with the crescent-shaped scar on his right cheek. He had not saved the thirteen men who washed up on Sicily's coast a couple of weeks back and he had never once wondered whether one of them had a distinguishing mark or if another was wearing a ring cast in the form of a sleeping snake. He had let their deaths wash over him, letting them retreat back out to sea and sink without a trace.

The woman in the Armani jacket put the photograph back in her bag, zipped it up, and headed for the door.

"I'm sorry!" blurted the Optician suddenly, turning to face her. "I'm so sorry that . . ."

The woman stopped and looked at him for a long moment, confused. Then her face cleared. She heaved her bag onto her shoulder, nodded briefly at the Optician, and left.

That night he dreamed he was alone on a rowboat and that the water below him was thundering and thrashing as some huge sea beast reared up underneath. He clung to the wooden frame but he felt that the sides were as flimsy as popsicle sticks and as they snapped in his hands he could see thick coils of silver scales swishing through the holes in the boat and he knew that any moment the head of a giant serpent would emerge from the waves and bear down on him. And then a man with a scar on his right cheek appeared beside him blowing a whistle saying it was over. It was over.

He woke up to Teresa's screaming.

CHAPTER 11

Galata was fretful in the harbor, creaking and seesawing with the other boats, pulling on her mooring as the buffeting wind unsettled the sea beneath her. The Optician watched her straining to break free of the marina. Like them, she had been turned back before she was ready; like them she had left a job half finished. He imagined she was yearning to be back in the open water to pick up the search again. He stroked her keel roughly as he might pet a dog. It was over, the Coast Guard captain had signaled, crossing and uncrossing his arms. The search was over. But it would never be over for them.

He told Teresa he was going to the post office. It was not exactly a lie. He did have a faulty batch of contact lenses he needed to ship back to Naples and there were some checks that needed sending but he knew that as soon as that was done he would wind up here at the port to spend a quiet moment with *Galata*. He told himself that he was doing it for Francesco. He'd check on the boat to give Francesco peace of mind now that he was back in Milan in the carpentry workshop. Yes, it was for Francesco that he'd come.

There was no one else around. The sullen afternoon sun, choked behind a cloak of heavy clouds strained to pick out a few steely glints from the thick and murky light-starved water. Even the fresh white paint of *Galata*'s cabin seemed grubby in the dirty light. He stepped tentatively onto her deck and felt her rock beneath his weight. She had been stripped for the winter: her cushions, flares, fenders, and dock lines were all stored inside and out of the way of the elements. Her gunwale gaped where the lifebuoy was usually attached. He looked down at the stern step and his hands immediately clenched into fists.

He was lonely without Francesco. He was lonely without all of them. He could see them all now again as he scanned *Galata*'s deck. The girl in the oil-slicked turquoise T-shirt sitting aloof there at the stern like a tragic figurehead. The teenage boy who'd made a diaper out of Teresa's reddish-orange

T-shirt, sobbing as he'd traced with his oily finger the number of passengers for them on the wooden boards.

Here on *Galata*'s deck the migrants—briefly—had all been safe. Now he feared they would be clutching at long, tangled lines of slippery asylum bureaucracy and that their grip would never be sure again. The email that Francesco had eventually received from one of the young men had been confused and unnerving. They were in a big holding camp in Sicily, the boy said, and they had each been given a number. The Optician sat down on the hard bench and hooked his finger over the elastic top of his sock, letting it snap back against his ankle bone. Camps and numbers did not give him peace of mind.

He ran the ball of his thumb along the gunwale, remembering how the bones of their knuckles had jutted out as they had clung there in shock. He needed them around him. He had come to understand that somehow when their hands had locked into his, it wasn't just them who had been pulled back into life. Up there on the cabin roof he had opened his eyes wide and he had seen them for the first time. The black dots that were not black dots but men, women, and children, flesh and bone and blood. He had stared into their eyes, which were rolling on the very cusp between life and death and he had not seen strangers. He had recognized their need and he had understood. The Optician had begun to see.

He rubbed the tip of his sneaker against an encrusted seagull dropping on the scrubbed deck. The rubber toecap juddered against the wood and sent pins and needles shooting up his calf and set his teeth on edge. All his senses seemed to be overly sharpened these days. At lunch time he had not been able to eat the chickpeas in the salad Teresa made because he could taste the aluminium of the can on their skin. They were the same brand they always used, she protested, fishing the tin from the trash to show him, but the metallic tang coated his tongue like blood and he could not swallow them. When she clanged the trash can lid back down in frustration and threw the salad tongs into the sink, he flinched at the ringing noise that echoed through the kitchen. He took off his glasses and pressed the heels of his hands into his eyes. The greasy smear of the sun against the thick clouds made his bloodshot eyeballs ache and each glint that refracted from the water's surface sliced through his pupils like a jagged knife.

Teresa seemed to float through the days, numbed. She drifted in and out of the apartment in a daze, walking into the bedroom to pick something up and then forgetting what it was and stumbling out again with the unsteady and confused gait of a sleepwalker. The doctor said she was suffering from deep shock; they'd had to visit the hospital several times. She looked at everything now with a detached interest like it didn't really matter much in her own world.

He imagined that her thoughts were piling up like the marbled white beach stones that filled the decorative glass jar in the bathroom. Somehow she was managing to push the most terrible thoughts to the bottom but what would happen to her if the stones suddenly shifted? He felt frightened for her. If he were honest, he felt a little frightened of her, too. He had always known who Teresa was and how she would react. She would cry when he was sharp with her, she would light up when he told her one of the boys was on the phone, she would blush like a schoolgirl when he whispered to her over a crowded dinner table that she looked beautiful. But since that day on the water she had become as unreadable as a cat. She slinked around the apartment not needing him and it made him nervous.

He needed her help more than ever, downstairs in the shop. He kept forgetting things like courtesy calls and the paperwork was getting muddled. He had done nothing about marking down sunglasses for an end of season sale. He knew he'd make a loss on those frames now; last year that would have kept him awake at night doing the mental arithmetic, but he could not make it matter anymore. He hadn't looked at the accounts for a week.

A few journalists still circled like vultures. The red-haired reporter came around to his shop yesterday when he was out, hounding Teresa, offering money for the "exclusive story." He was deeply offended about the money when Teresa told him. Was that how people saw him? A ruthless opportunist who would trade the testimonies of the desperate for a few gold pieces?

And he despised the pejorative word "story" they used to describe the tragedy. It made the shipwreck seem like a once-upon-a-time fable that you might tell to children at bedtime. He picked at a speck of white paint on the metal gunwale. Well, there would be no happily ever after, not for the dead, not for the survivors, not for them.

Out of the whole crew, it was only he and Teresa left on the island now. The little gathering Francesco organized every year to say goodbye to the group had been subdued this time although the Optician noticed they all drank more wine than usual. Elena got touchy with an inattentive waiter and Matteo's clowning was so forced and half-hearted that only the good-natured Maria continued to laugh. Everyone's face bore the heavy, dark footprints of their disturbed nights. The pouches under Giulia's eyes were so pronounced that he asked her if a mosquito had bitten her. She became very teary during the meal. After they ate, he, Francesco, and Gabriele sat on the terrace smoking endless ciga-rettes together. They said very little but the silence was comforting and companionable. Just the eight of them. Just the eight.

He decided to text Francesco, to tell him that the old lady was doing fine. He said that they had just been strolling, just taking a walk by the quay-side, when they'd made a quick detour to check up on *Galata* after the recent rainstorm. All good, he texted. Everything's good here, fine and dandy. Francesco's reply came back quickly. Are you OK? he asked.

He felt foolish really but he climbed up on the roof of the wheelhouse anyway. Back to his old lookout post. His eyes smarted as he strained to look down deep into the water of the harbor. A shoal of small silvery blue fish flitted between the snug boats, discernible only intermittently as they zig-zagged through the shards of sporadic sunlight. He took off his glasses and let the images around him blur and the colors bleed and run into one another. The myopic world was a softer one, an indistinct jumble of shapes and forms with no edges.

But he could not ignore the fact that the waving hands had always been visible to him. They waved in the water, yes, but they also waved from the reception center, from the church steps, and from the roadside where he had jogged past them, blindly. They waved from the newspaper columns and from the television screens where he filtered them out and switched them off. They were always in his line of vision and he had chosen not to see them.

He checked his watch and realized he'd have to walk back quickly to make his four o'clock at the shop. He grimaced. Mr. Abate the crabby old boatman who rented out a fleet of *pedalos* to the tourists in high season. Never exactly a pleasure. He swung himself down from the cabin roof and stood silently for a moment or two, listening to the boats complaining, before climbing back onto the quayside.

On the way home, he crossed over the road to pause at the migrant boat graveyard where a flotilla of wooden cadavers were marooned on the gravel, their hulls splintered with unsightly wounds. The worn-out vessels were lying heavily on their sides as if in a gesture of surrender. He winced, looking at them. How many years now had desperate people washed up here, drained of every last drop of their strength? He clenched his jaw. And how many more smashed wrecks would it take before Europe stopped debating and instead agreed to do something? The cawing gulls, wheeling and gliding on the warm thermals, tormented his ears.

Mr. Abate was early for his appointment and when the Optician walked into the shop he was already grumbling to Teresa about something. The Optician forced his face into an unwilling smile and greeted him professionally. The old man was slightly deaf and the pitch of his voice grated.

He talked incessantly through his tonometry test as the Optician tried to measure the pressure inside his eyes.

"Puff of air coming now, Mr. Abate."

He picked up his ophthalmoscope and moved closer to Mr. Abate.

"Try and hold still for me, Mr. Abate," he said gently. "I'm just trying to get a look at your optic nerve to check if it's as healthy as the rest of you." But the old man grumbled on.

Not a single repeat booking in his brother's hotel, he said. First time ever since they'd started up the place thirty-five years back that clients had checked out at the reception desk and hadn't immediately asked to reserve the same room for next year. Too worried, they said. Too worried that they might swim into a dead body! Damned migrants were turning this paradise island into a horror story!

The Optician drew back his head and closed his own eyes briefly. The vein above his right ear throbbed. As he opened his eyes he saw that Teresa was standing diagonally on the threshold of the shop, her left hand flat against her ear to block out Mr. Abate. She was doing that chewing and pursing thing with her mouth that he knew meant tears.

A few years back, Mr. Abate continued, a few years back his brother's hotel had a waiting list as long as your arm for rooms; now the reservation book was blank. Damn migrants were ruining Lampedusa; everyone was choosing Sardinia these days for their holidays although they all knew they'd get fleeced over there. Price of a *pedalo* in Sardinia was double what he charged here in August. More than double! They'd driven away trade, those migrants. They'd driven away trade.

The Optician could smell mackerel on the old man's breath. He was careful always to clean his own teeth after lunch.

"Eyes wide open now, Mr. Abate, please."

Got to stop everyone talking about the migrants, Mr. Abate said. That's the problem, you see. Everyone's focus is on the migrants. Every concert held on the island is a fundraiser for the migrants, every newspaper story that mentions Lampedusa is about the migrants. Well, it's time to change the record!

"All looking good, Mr. Abate," soothed the Optician as one hand clenched into a fist behind his back. Teresa was still on the doorstep. Her neck was flushed and her chin was tilted upward. He was reminded of the girl in the turquoise T-shirt who had been too proud to cry on the boat.

He cleared his throat. "Now I'd like to test your peripheral vision quickly," he said courteously. "Could you please concentrate on the light spots I'm going to show you and call out when you see one?"

Not even our problem, muttered the old man as he positioned himself forward in the chair. Not even our problem, and yet everywhere you look, they're in your face.

"It's important you tell me when you see the light spots, Mr. Abate."

What's it got to do with us anyway? What have any of these people got to do with us?

"Mr. Abate? The light spots!"

A door slammed and they both jumped at the loud bang. The Optician looked up sharply and was just in time to see Teresa run past the window in the direction of Giulia's shop, her face beetroot red from suppressed crying. The Optician took off his glasses and massaged his eyes, breathing out slowly. She must have forgotten that Giulia and Gabriele left Lampedusa last week.

"What was that?" said Mr. Abate, fumbling on the table for his glasses. "What the hell was that?"

The Optician pushed his own glasses back onto the bridge of his nose and rubbed his hands together.

"Just the wind, Mr. Abate," he said reassuringly as he steered the old gentleman's head back toward the chin rest. "Just the wind."

CHAPTER 12

If the wind had picked up. If the wind had not stayed soft. If the wind had begun to needle the sea until it raged in fury. If.

How many times had he tortured himself with the "if" game over the last twelve months? A year on and he still played it at night in his head when he could not sleep, he played it staring at his computer in the office, he played it walking to the post office, he played it in the waiting room at the airport. And it played him. Over and over.

If the wind had suddenly picked up, Francesco would have called the shop to warn them that it would be an uncomfortable cruise with the sea so choppy. Best to postpone till next week, he would have said. If he had tripped on that loose paving stone on Via Roma on the run home and had sprained his ankle, he could not have boarded the boat on crutches. If Maria had never phoned about going out for dinner and instead they had chanced the last of the sardines at the fishmongers, perhaps he and Teresa would both have had terrible food poisoning and he would have called Francesco from his bed to make their excuses. If he had not boarded that boat on that day he would have spent the weekend marking down last season's sunglasses and setting up a sale. Now, a full year on and he might have made a little profit, perhaps he would be surprising his boy by putting a few hundred euros into his account to help with the launch of his new business. The circles beneath his eyes would not be bruised by dark shadows, he would sleep easily at night, and his wife would not wake up screaming, unable to breathe. If.

Wait! He was not the only player in this game. What about them? whispers the voice in his head. Where does this new narrative leave the refugees and their waving hands? If he had not boarded that boat on that day, they would still have boarded theirs. They would have still capsized and ended up in the water. So look! There they are in the waves screaming and yet now there is no one to hear them. They're waving and they're clutching at hands that are not there. Hands that will not come, hands that will never come because they're busy dialing Mrs. Maggiorani reminding her of her sight test next week and busy putting sale stickers on the ladies' sunglasses.

No. The cards had been dealt out already and there would be no reshuffling of the pack. He would accept his hand and play it out; he would not choose to sit out the game and simply watch. It was just that sometimes he wished his head could be still again, the way it had been before they took the boat trip. When his thoughts were not constantly rising and falling like the swell of the sea, searching for answers, continually tossing questions and flinging "ifs" and "buts" at him until he wanted to weep with exhaustion. Because you know, if he had only . . .

For pity's sake! He turned on the cold tap at the sink and stuck his face under the icy stream until his breath came in gasps. Get over yourself, he muttered as he searched for the towel. Get over yourself because you are where you are. He rubbed the condensation off the mirror with a corner of the towel and flicked it over his shoulder. And anyway, he reminded himself as he picked up his razor, today was the first anniversary of the shipwreck, and it would be a good day as well as a sad day. It would be a good day because three of those refugees they rescued were coming back to the island and they would see each other again. He checked his watch. In two hours, they would be reunited. Less than two hours. He felt a tide of excitement and he felt nerves knot in his stomach

Was that Teresa singing? The Optician put down his razor curiously and opened the bathroom door a little, putting his ear to the crack. Yes, it was definitely Teresa's voice accompanying Madonna on the radio in the bedroom opposite. He peered through the little gap. He could see her now too as she was making the bed, plumping up the pillows in time to the beat, dancing a little. There was lightness in her movements, almost joy.

"La la la, la la la la la . . ."

He smiled and shut the door quickly before she realized she was being watched and became self-conscious. Let her have a carefree moment! This last year had taken its toll on her; the nightmares haunted her through the winter and her appetite had deserted her. But she'd begun to pick up considerably when Maria and Gabriele and Giulia had reappeared at the start of the new season, along with the warm weather. Occasionally he still woke up to her scrabbling at the sheets, unable to draw breath and he knew then she was again in the water with them, struggling to stay afloat. But during the summer her laugh had come back and now she was singing.

"La la la, la la la la la!"

Of course, the tune was inane. How did people get paid for such preposterous rubbish? He was surprised when he picked up his razor again to realize he was also singing it. He grinned foolishly. At least Matteo hadn't witnessed that!

He felt suddenly light himself as he trimmed the little salt-and-pepper goatee beard he now wore. He still had the dark rings under his eyes and his face was decidedly thinner. He'd also lost weight over the year; those beige trousers he'd bought toward the end of last summer hung on him now. Teresa said he looked liked he'd borrowed his father's trousers. Yet he still felt strong, especially on a day like today. He shrugged back his shoulders and flexed the muscles in his chest. He must keep calm and keep his emotions under control. He needed to manage this properly for Teresa. Pushing open the bathroom door, he was startled by her pirouetting across the landing. They both laughed.

It was a gray morning and the sky was surly but it was still warm enough to sit outside on the cafe terrace. Almost as soon as they sat down,

Maria, Matteo, and Francesco arrived and the Optician could feel a swell of excitement rise up in him. Francesco had spent the last three days working like a dog on the boat, touching up her paintwork, washing salt stains from her cushion covers, scrubbing the sea slime off her fenders. Now the old girl was ready, said Francesco, to welcome them like kings. That afternoon the eight of them would take the survivors back on the water to the spot of the shipwreck. There would be a ceremony to remember those they could not save. Maria bought flowers to throw into the sea. She told them her kitchen was alight with the yellow and white blooms. The Optician folded his paper napkin into squares, taking care to align the two sides of the serviette accurately.

It wasn't that he was nervous about being on the water. He was a man of the sea, for pity's sake, saltwater was in his blood! He had sailed countless times since the shipwreck, both here and back in Naples. He'd helmed yachts, he'd been out on pleasure cruises, and this summer he and Francesco had often taken *Galata* on fishing trips to the cove off Rabbit Beach. OK, he would admit he scanned the waves a little more attentively than before but he never felt panicked or anything. Today, though, would be the first time that all eight of them would be back out there together. All eight on board *Galata*. And in spite of the excitement there was an unsettling portent about that. There was just this feeling that history might choose to repeat itself somehow, a fear that the sea might decide to throw them another challenge.

He tore the napkin down the middle. He must be going soft. It was enough that he'd been singing along to Madonna this morning; was he going to become superstitious now, too?

Giulia and Gabriele arrived with Elena in tow. Elena craned her neck to look at the pastries displayed on the counter inside. She wandered inside to make a more informed choice. The Optician glanced at his watch again and warned them they would not have time to linger over their coffee now if they were to get to the town hall by ten-thirty. Giulia gave him a playful kick under the table and told him to lighten up. But we can't be late for the refugees, he wanted to insist. It's like when we saw them at the airport hangar for the memorial service. We need to be there at the moment of their arrival so they will know that we are anxious to see them, so they'll know that all these months we have been waiting for them. He said nothing but his left leg bounced nervously under the table.

Francesco was talking about the conference that was to be held at the town hall before the ceremony at sea; it was a conference, he explained, to look at what had been learned from the October 3 tragedy. Elena and Giulia said they would be interested to sit in on it but the Optician screwed up his face in distaste. He shied away from such public gatherings. It was all hot air anyway and it would just irritate him and get him worked up. A roomful of official bleeding hearts from Italy and the EU saying how awful it was that shipwrecks were still occurring, shaking their heads over last month's tragedy where five hundred people were drowned off the coast of Malta. Yes, it was awful, so what were they actually doing about it? He drummed his fingers on the table. It had been barely a year since the Italian Navy had launched its special search-and-rescue mission, Mare Nostrum, and already the government was announcing its closure, saying it was too costly to run without the help of their European neighbors. No. It was best he did not attend the conference. He could not stomach any more of their empty promises. Teresa put a hand on his jiggling knee to still him.

He took a deep breath. Anyway, this was to be a happy day, a day for celebration! Elena had bought a selection of cakes and sweet biscuits and was pressing them on the group. She dug him in the ribs.

"You could do with fattening up a bit," she teased him, proffering the plate. He studied the cakes carefully and selected a small almond biscuit. It was still warm from the oven and crumbled in his mouth, making him cough. They laughed at him as the tears rolled down his cheeks.

Maria brought out the letter they had all received from the town hall with the program of events. The survivors and some of the relatives of the dead arrived on the island last night, she read aloud, having met the Pope in Rome. After the conference this morning there would be a light lunch and then the special ceremony would take place with a flotilla of boats making a pilgrimage to the site. He grimaced at that. Call him selfish, but he wished they could filter out all these official engagements and just enjoy the private moments with the survivors alone. He knew the others felt the same. He could see Gabriele scowling. Francesco looked up at the sky and clicked his tongue disapprovingly. There would be rain later, he warned. You could feel it coming.

He took Teresa's arm on the way to the town hall and squeezed it against his. He needed this reunion to be healing for her. He hoped it would be healing for all of them. Just in front of the mayor's office, they met some friends of Elena's from a local NGO who were planning a demonstration. He looked at their placards and leaned down to see the half-furled banners they made from old sheets. "Every day is October 3," the signs read.

Inside the town hall their names were ticked off a long list by a harassed employee who kept dropping her pen as she tried to leaf through the pages on her clipboard. She motioned to the heavy oak door on her right. Everyone is in there, she said. In that room.

The Optician was nearest the door. He hesitated, his fingers curled around the handle, his heart pounding. He turned and looked at his friends as his hand pushed down. Their faces were charged with excitement and fear and he saw that they all needed this to be a success as much as he did. How ironic that they had come to need so much from these refugees who had nothing! Sometimes in his dreams, the hands he saw waving now in the water were white, not black at all. He nodded at his friends. The door handle went down but he still could not quite push the door open. It was Teresa who got it open in the end.

The room was small and full of middle-aged white men in suits and young East Africans wearing T-shirts, jeans, and tennis shoes. Beside the long trestle table at the back of the room, a table laid with jugs of fruit juice and coffee urns, the Optician spotted one of the fishermen who helped *Galata* with the rescue. He was spruced up in a brown corduroy jacket. His red hand was huge on the little espresso cup he was holding. But the Optician did not have time to observe any more.

The young man, the first one they had rescued, was in Teresa's arms almost instantaneously, and they hugged each other like a mother and son. After a few seconds, the boy pulled away from her, chattering excitedly, wanting to show her something.

"Look!" he said, cuddling a piece of material to his chin like a child with a comforter. "Look!" The Optician recognized it immediately. It was the bright orange T-shirt that Teresa had given the young man when he had been dragged naked aboard *Galata,* the one he had worn like a pair of pants. Teresa cupped the teenager's face in her hands. How humbling that this boy should have kept it, that after all this time and after God knows how many refugee camps and asylum centers, he still had it!

He treasured Teresa's kindness. The Optician pulled the boy to him quickly so he could not see him weep.

Maria and Gabriele were exclaiming over a piece of paper that the other two refugees had given them. The oldest of the survivors, a man perhaps in his early thirties, had learned a few words of Italian and explained to them that they wanted to bring a gift for the people who had saved their lives. It was not much, he said with a little shrug of embarrassment, but it had been done—he touched his heart—with all their love. The Optician bent over the paper. It was a simple but beautifully executed drawing of a grasping hand coming out of the water being met by another hand which clasped it in a fierce grip. It was the summary of their history.

The oldest survivor, they learned over coffee, had been a teacher in Eritrea. It was not a good job, he made them understand, to teach children who had no future. Through his limited Italian and their poor English they pieced together the refugees' story; it was like doing a difficult crossword puzzle with everyone chipping in and guessing the answers to the clues. The Optician had to concentrate hard to follow. He grasped that all three survivors were living in Sweden now, that most of those who were rescued were living there, waiting for their asylum claims to be processed so they would be able to work and start new lives. They were a little frustrated that their lives were on pause while the paperwork went through. Sweden was beautiful and very cold, they said, but they were not complaining. The Optician cut in with an apologetic wave of his hand. What about the girl? he asked eagerly. What had happened to the girl, the girl in the turquoise T-shirt? The three men conferred among themselves for a moment in their own language. Norway? they suggested. Maybe Norway? The Optician felt his shoulders sink.

The woman with the clipboard came into the room and made an announcement that the conference would start shortly. Francesco explained to the three men that they would see them at the port for the ceremony at sea, reassuring them that he would take them in his boat, that they would all be together. The young man who was still clutching Teresa's T-shirt shuffled nervously from foot to foot, chewing his lip. He was very frightened, the other two explained. He almost had not come because he was so scared of being on the sea again. The Optician took the teenager's hand, balled it into a fist, clasped his own on top of it, and then pointed toward the drawing. The boy looked for a second or two into the Optician's eyes as if searching for something and then his face relaxed. He nodded to the Optician, trusting him.

It was late afternoon by the time they cast off and the sky was still unsure whether to dump its heavy rain clouds or not. The Optician scanned the sky suspiciously. Maria and Teresa were seated on a bench on deck, each holding a hand of the nervous young man. The first time he had taken Teresa out to sea after the shipwreck she had been white with motion sickness. Now, fussing over this boy she helped save, she looked content. He began to relax.

The teacher stopped talking almost as soon as they boarded *Galata*. He moved toward the prow of the boat where he stood with his face to the wind, staring straight ahead. The other young man, his baseball cap pulled low over his forehead, sat beside the lifebuoy, one hand raised and stroking its coiled rope. The Optician nudged the young man's foot with his own and gave him the thumbs-up sign. The young man returned the gesture with a small smile.

On each side of *Galata* the Coast Guard and fishing vessels flanked them, rocking the boat a little with their wake.

He felt shame when they reached the shipwreck site. Shame that they were so ludicrously close to shore. The point of the coastline looked vulgar jutting out into the sea like that. He imagined how the shoreline must have taunted the migrants while they were drowning in the water, flaunting its proximity and parading the promise of its harbor. They were barely a kilometer from land, and yet three hundred and sixty-eight people had died here. He covered his face with his hands and felt Gabriele grip his shoulder.

The Coast Guard vessel gave two long blasts on its horn: the sign that the ceremonies should begin. *Galata*'s crew had not planned anything specific themselves although it was understood that if anyone would speak, it must be Francesco. But the Optician saw that the three survivors had rehearsed what they should do. Each of them picked up a bouquet of Maria's sunny flowers and turned to face the water. They began to pray in their own language, half-chanting, half-singing, steadying themselves against the sea's gait with one hip lodged between the bars of the gunwale. Then with a cry they threw the flowers into the sea and the Optician saw the oldest survivor take something that looked like coarse sand or perhaps rice from the pocket of his jeans and distribute it between them. They recited some more verses together and scattered the grains into the waves, their heads bowed.

He watched their backs convulsing with sobs and again he was reminded of them at the aircraft hangar in their pitiful secondhand cast-off clothes and ill-matched shoes. He saw the gleaming coffins, spaced out with military precision, the cheerful teddy bears propped up on the tiny white caskets, the girl with her blistered fingers and the stink of her burned-out, ruined life. And he saw the young man wearing Teresa's vermillion T-shirt bunched round his waist like a diaper, howling like a helpless new-born, slithering onto the deck in his afterbirth of oil and gasoline.

The same young man turned from the sea and faced him, holding out his hand.

"Come," he said, looking him squarely in the eye. "Come and be with us."

So they joined hands, all of them and stood in a line, looking out across the sea. And when the refugees began to pray again he did not feel uncomfortable. His right hand held the teenager's hand. In his left, he clutched Teresa's hand. He no longer saw the Coast Guard and the press boats and the fishing vessels that surrounded them. He just felt them, and only them, and stillness. And suddenly he knew with absolute clarity that he was living in the most pure and intimate moment of his life. He could feel the collective pulse of all of them, of his dearest friends and these refugees, throbbing in his own wrists. He could feel their shared lifeline.

The teenager turned to him, let go of his hand, and held up his index finger.

"Today," he said, "I am one year old."

He pointed to the Optician and then to the sea. In there, he was trying to say, jabbing his finger at the water, I was dead. But here—he swept his arms across *Galata*'s deck—here, I was reborn.

The first spots of rain were falling as they got back to port. This time, though, when the three survivors climbed down onto the quayside there were no tears when saying goodbye. Tomorrow afternoon they would see each other again and no one would try to stop them. So they parted with smiles and bear hugs, sure of each other, like family. But he still watched as they wandered away until he saw that they met up with the other survivors and were safe.

It was pretty much dark by the time they sorted out *Galata* and fixed her back safely at her mooring. Gabriele said he needed a beer. Matteo replied he needed two beers. That's when the rain came, rupturing all the clouds on them at once and forcing them to run for cover. And that's why the Optician ended up in that awful bar he hated with the crude electric lighting and the irritating music.

The first beer very quickly became two. And then, when the Optician checked his watch it turned out to be very much *aperitivi* time and it would be a crime really not to raise a glass of wine to the day.

What was that song they were playing? Was it that same Madonna track? He nudged Teresa.

"'La la la la la,'" he mimed and they both started laughing.

"You're more chilled out," said Maria, giving his knee a fond squeeze. "Did you know that, Mr. Fastidiousness? You're more chilled out these days."

He knocked the wine back to make a point.

A few wispy clouds lingered in the night sky as they left the bar, veiling the moon in a sheer film. There was no wind to shift the clouds. The Optician felt the alcohol swirl pleasantly around his brain as he tipped his head back to stare at the stars.

Maria linked arms with him. He offered his left arm to Teresa, who in turn held out her left elbow to Francesco. The Optician grinned as Giulia threaded her arm under Francesco's sleeve and snaked her left hand into Matteo's coat pocket. They walked like that, toward Via Roma, a human chain, arm in arm and laughing wildly. Just the eight of them. Just the eight.

"Hey," he said, nudging his hip into Maria's and looking across Teresa to Francesco. "If the wind stays soft, how about we take *Galata* out tomorrow night so we can wake up to a sunrise on the water on Sunday morning? An October mini-break?"

A murmur of approval moved from one end of the line to the other.

"Just the eight of us," said the Optician. "If the wind stays soft."

EPILOGUE

You ask me why I don't give interviews. You ask me why I don't like to tell this story. But if I still cannot believe it really happened, how can you? If I talk about it your jaw will drop and you will say but how did you, how could you? It is impossible for you to understand. Only the eight of us can really understand. You see, we were eight on that boat. Just eight. With one rubber ring.

I saw them every day and yet I did not see them. I did not reach out.

Forty-seven. We saved forty-seven. But we couldn't save them all.

I was never trying to be a hero. I'm humbled by what happened on the water. I'm humbled. I just remember the hands in mine, the fingers cemented into mine. And of course I remember the hands that slipped away.

That's when the nightmares crawl back. The oily, slippery hands vanishing under the water, the animalistic screams that were not seagulls, muffled then swallowed by the waves. We are all haunted by them.

I was on the sea that day. And I don't rule out that it could be me on the sea again tomorrow. There will be another time, another boat. There will be more hands, more bodies thrashing, more voices begging. Every time I am on the sea now I'm searching for them, scouring, breathless.

If the wind had picked up. If the wind had not stayed soft. If the wind had begun to needle the sea until it raged in fury. If.

Cypherpunks
Freedom and the Future of
the Internet
JULIAN ASSANGE with
JACOB APPELBAUM, ANDY
MÜLLER-MAGUHN, AND
JÉRÉMIE ZIMMERMANN

When Google Met
Wikileaks
JULIAN ASSANGE

Kingdom of the Unjust
Behind the U.S.–Saudi
Connection
MEDEA BENJAMIN

A Narco History
How the US and Mexico
Jointly Created the "Mexican
Drug War"
CARMEN BOULLOSA AND
MIKE WALLACE

Beautiful Trouble
A Toolbox for Revolution
ASSEMBLED BY ANDREW
BOYD WITH DAVE OSWALD
MITCHELL

Bowie
SIMON CRITCHLEY

Extinction
A Radical History
ASHLEY DAWSON

Black Ops Advertising
Native Ads, Content
Marketing, and the Covert
World of the Digital Sell
MARA EINSTEIN

Beautiful Solutions
A Toolbox for Liberation
EDITED BY ELI FEGHALI,
RACHEL PLATTUS, AND
ELANDRIA WILLIAMS

Remembering Akbar
Inside the Iranian Revolution
BEHROOZ GHAMARI

Folding the Red into the
Black
or Developing a Viable
*Un*topia for Human Survival in
the 21st Century
WALTER MOSLEY

Inferno
(A Poet's Novel)
EILEEN MYLES

Finks
How the CIA Tricked the
World's Best Writers
JOEL WHITNEY

Trump Unveiled
Exposing the Bigoted
Billionaire
JOHN K. WILSON